Once Upon an

Modern Fairy Tal

Compiled and edited by

Kaye Lynne Booth

WordCrafter Press

Introduction by Kaye Lynne Booth

Compiled and edited by Kaye Lynne Booth

WC

Cover by ***WordCrafter Press***

Table of Contents

Introduction

In the fall of 2021, I was privileged to be a part of the *Gilded Glass* editorial team for Western State Colorado University and *WordFire Press*. It was quite an experience really, to read through over six hundred short fiction submissions. We were looking for stories that fit our theme and criteria, were well crafted and thought provoking, and near ready for publication, requiring only minimal editing. When you have only two semesters to run through the entire publication process for an anthology, you don't have the time for extensive editing on twenty to twenty-five stories. But as the months of the fall semester dwindled down, we ran a couple of elimination rounds and eventually, in one two and a half hour long Zoom call, selected twenty-two stories to be included in the anthology, including stories from five big name authors, which was very cool.

But it wasn't easy. There were so many stories which were really good, which had to be rejected, because they didn't quite fit the criteria, or just because there were others that were better, and there just wasn't room within our budget to include more. However, as a small independent publisher myself, I just couldn't bear to let some of these excellent tales be tossed to the side, when they really were good enough to find publication. There were many stories which I couldn't bring myself to let go of.

Instead, I downloaded those stories and the authors' contact information, and I extended invitations to have these story gems published in a different anthology, after the final decisions had been made for *Gilded Glass* and all rejection and acceptance letters had been sent out, of course. Some of the stories I saved fit the fairy tale theme well, while others may have had interesting incorporation of the mirror element and not so much emphasis on the folkloric aspects, and there were some stories which really didn't fit either. Because of this, it was difficult to think of about a theme, although they did have certain things in common. What I came up with was enough stories to do three separately themed anthologies.

Fairy tales and folklore are a special kind of fantasy; the kind that takes you to magical lands, where anything is possible, and even evil curses can be overcome. They are filled with beautiful princesses and handsome princes, old hags and cagey witches, castles to be conquered, damsels to be rescued, and spells to be broken. I mean, what's not to like?

Once Upon an Ever After is a collection of fairy tales, or fairy tale-like stories, salvaged from the slush pile, because I thought they were too good to be discarded. It's a lovely and diverse collection of modern fairy tales and folklore. I do hope you'll enjoy them. And now....

Be prepared to be enchanted...

The Mirror of Truth (And Other Arcane Artefacts)

By Charlie Emrys

To say the ruins of the Dark Enchanter's castle dominated the skyline would be a kind overstatement. Rather, they slumped against the horizon like a hard-worked maidservant who, on her stumbling way to bed after a long day of toil, had instead collapsed into sleep against her chamber door.

The castle was once an impenetrable fortress, commanding unparalleled views across the coast of the queendom of Iriring. From here, it was said the Dark Enchanter had launched her decades-long reign of evil.

But, as reigns are wont to do, the Dark Enchanter's ended, not with a bang, but with several controlled explosions. The aptly named Definitely Final Battle brought the Dark Enchanter, and her fortress, to rubble.

It was fear at first, in the aftermath, that kept most of the surrounding townsfolk away from the ruins. Time succeeded with the rest. Now, precious few set foot on the flagstones that had once borne the steps of the queendom's most infamous tyrant. And even fewer still remembered the treasures buried within.

For deep in the ruins of the castle, sunk under moss and leaf rot and toppled stone, there lay a once-magnificent chamber. And in this chamber, the Dark Enchanter had kept all her artefacts of incredible magical power; the power-sapping basilisk staff; Chartra, the green-fire griffin, bane of lost travelers; the terrible formless hoard-beast. Yet not one of these came close to her most prized possession, the thing believed to be the source of all her power, the very item that had delivered her to the throne – the Mirror of Truth.

It rests there still. At least, that's what the stories tell, if any cared to listen.

"BE NOT AFRAID, BRAVE little one. Come closer..."

The voice was sibylline, silky, silver. It seemed to come from nowhere in particular-yet commanded all attention. Young as fresh snow, ancient as glaciers, it called.

"It has been, oh, *so* long since I had visitors. Do you know what it is I can grant you, little adventurer?"

The chamber was cold. Here and there weak sunlight broke through tumbled earth and stone, like distant heatless stars. Ash, settled for decades, stirred by a footstep.

"I can grant you your most secret desire. That ache you keep locked in your heart, that wish you'd never spoken aloud, that dream that keeps you from sleep... come to me, and I will show it to you. I will make it true."

A quiet sigh, perhaps wistful, broke the air. Footsteps, timid, then more certain. Upon the remains of a dais, pale light glinted on metal, sending dazzling sparks across the floor.

"That's right, my new companion, now let me see your face—"

The stranger stepped into the light. And coo'ed.

"- oh not another *bloody* pigeon!"

Groans filled the chamber.

"Not again!"

"How do the damn things keep getting in?"

"RARAGHGHG!!"

"Yes. Well put, Dragor, it *is* a right nuisance."

A torch flared alight with a burst of green sparks, throwing the shadows from the room. It was clutched in the weather-worn talons of a fierce stone griffin, with eyes the same unseemly green and a lower body fused to a collapsed wall. In front of the griffin, its light illuminated a half-burnt staff coiled about by a fearsome basilisk, which in turn, leant against a chest of age-dulled coins that shifted now and then, like something underneath was breathing.

The pigeon, startled by the sudden noise and movement, took flight, aiming for what seemed to be a patch of clear night sky- and promptly knocked itself out against the surface of a mirror.

"Ow!" the Mirror of Truth exclaimed. "Couldn't it see I'm right here? I'm not exactly hard to miss." Though it lacked limbs, the Mirror gave a sense that it was gesturing to itself.

Its huge gilt frame was as tall as an imposing woman, and though the silver was tarnished, it still shimmered impressively in the torchlight. It was etched with a filigree of tiny figures, marvelous in their detail, and there had been a time where mages and scholars the world over would beg to study those intricate pictograms, to trace the patterns of its metal.

Now the Mirror was studied only by spiderlings, looking to string a web and touched only by the greasy bodies of confused pigeons.

"I'm going to stink like a bird for a decade now," the Mirror said.

"Now there's no call for that," said the griffin, shifting the torch in her claws. "I'm half-bird on my mother's side, you know."

The Mirror continued, ignoring her. "Not that there's anyone here to notice how I smell." All at once, its surface grew clouded and reflected the image of a miserable grey drizzle.

"Two centuries she's been gone, leaving us all to rot down here." The griffin complained. "And not a single soul has even bothered to pillage her most prized possessions! I mean, what? Do tools of immense arcane power mean nothing to people anymore?"

Coins scattered from the ancient chest. "I know. It's almost like no one *wants* to be cursed."

"We're not cursed," the Mirror snapped.

"And why else would we be left down here?" the griffin asked, picking her beak with a long talon.

The Mirror sighed.

"Perhaps we are forgotten."

Rain pattered across its surface.

NADIM WAS BEGINNING to think he had the wrong address. He looked again at the parcel in his hands—carefully wrapped in cloth, embroidered with sweet smiling puppies and addressed to 'dear little Roisin'—and out at the harsh wind-swept clifftop where he found himself. It didn't look like the kind of place you'd expect to find the farrier's cousin's niece's birthday party in full swing and, indeed, there didn't appear to be another human soul for miles.

Perhaps it's a surprise party, Nadim thought. A lone gull wailed above him.

Nadim had never got lost on a delivery before. Granted, that was because he'd never had to deliver a parcel further than a few streets down before, but he wasn't about to ruin that streak on his first inter-village delivery gig. He'd even bought a compass for the occasion, though he hadn't yet worked out how to use it.

So, he decided, he probably wasn't lost. Little Roisin's birthday party surely was happening here, if you broadened the sense of 'here' to mean 'somewhere within six miles of Nadim's current position'.

"Well, no harm in taking a little look around!" he said to no one in particular. "Who's to say the farrier's cousin doesn't live just behind that suspiciously stone-like mound?" The gull agreed with a high keen, or perhaps disagreed vehemently; Nadim didn't speak gull, but he was an optimist.

So, he made his way over the sparse, wind-blown grass, stone and rubble crunching beneath his boots. Somewhere far below and out of sight, the sea rumbled like a memory of a storm.

As he approached the mound, it became clear that it wasn't alone. The crumbling forms of foundations, walls, and staircases began to emerge from the gloom. He rounded the side of the mound that faced seaward and almost tripped. The ground here sloped down into a wide, hollow depression littered with charred stone and wood that had been smoothed into strange forms by the wind and salt air. Crows, gulls, and pigeons clamored about the ruins looking for perches, and grass and lichen grew over everything in patches, creating the sense that the whole site was sinking into a boggy green marsh.

Nadim was almost certain little Roisin didn't live here. Defeated, he was about to turn and begin the long march back to the main track when he heard a bird cry out in distress.

A pigeon had caught its foot in a crevice in the ground. It was a young one, with an absurdly oversized beak and downy feathers, and was squeaking forlornly as it tried and failed to free itself.

Nadim felt a certain kinship for pigeons. 'Nature's couriers', his mum called them. 'Weird-looking things,' said everyone else. His heart went out to the little one, and so did his feet.

"It's alright!" he called out to the forlorn bird as he picked his way down into the hollow. "I'm coming to rescue you!"

The ground beneath his feet was getting spongier as he got closer. He reached out his hand to the pigeon. Not quite close enough. He took another step, and this time he could grip the little animal gently in both hands.

"Easy does it," he said, and stepped back.

The ground gave way beneath him.

The pigeon fluttered to safety.

Nadim fell.

"GREAT LORDS OF IRIRITH, what in the *world* is happening?"

"GRARGHH?!"

"It's alright, Dragor, don't cry!"

A GREAT PLUME OF DUST, mud and termites rained down into the Dark Enchanter's secret chamber, shortly followed by a body, which landed with a winded *-ough*.

Chartri extended her torch towards the hole in the ceiling, then over the body on the floor.

"Well, would you look at that?" she exclaimed delightedly. "It's raining corpses. Just like in the old days!"

"I should be so lucky," said the hoard-beast. "What I wouldn't do for a good old-fashioned corpse-feast."

"Would everyone be quiet for a second?" the Mirror said. It reflected the glow from Chartri's torch across the floor, brightening the scene. "I don't think the creature's dead yet."

This was news to Nadim, who had been listening from the floor, convinced the demons of the next world surrounded him. He opened his eyes and flexed his legs a little, just to check they were still attached. One twinged painfully.

"You there, girl, get up!"

"I'm a man!" Nadim said automatically. He had, in fact, intended to say *aargh, oh god, a talking statue!* but in times of great mental stress, the brain does occasionally fall back on familiar scripts.

"Really? Are you sure?"

"I—*yes*, I'm sure. What a rude thing to ask!"

"If he says he's a man, then he's a man," interrupted the Mirror, who wasn't entirely sure what the difference was, either way. "I think there are more pressing questions here, like..." it adjusted itself, and an enigmatic, curved, delicate figure appeared in the glass. "What is your most secret desire? Your dream that keeps you awake? Your..."

"Your hidden truth, yeah, yeah, we've heard it all before, you old schemer." The hoard-beast shifted restlessly beneath his coins. "How come you get first dibs, eh? Just because you were the old girl's favourite? We're all starving for a soul down here. Speaking of which, boy! Come, take a coin!"

Nadim had been shakily pulling himself to his feet while trying—and largely failing — to ignore the pain in his leg. He now looked at the churning, roiling mass of stained metal that beckoned to him. "Um," he said. "I think I'll pass. Also, I'm 29, so not a boy."

"What is *wrong* with today's youth?" Chartri said. "No one comes down here for centuries, then when they do, they're all, *'oh, don't call me this, don't call me that! No, I don't want a cursed coin from a befanged treasure chest!'*" She shook her head, and her torch-flames glinted off the hook of her beak. "Things have really gone downhill since the Dark Enchanter was in charge."

"Grargghghg," said Dragor, baring his fangs at Nadim.

"Yes, well put, darling."

Nadim took a slow, calming, not at all hysterical breath, and channeled his best customer service voice. "I'm terribly sorry," he picked up the package for little Roisin where he had dropped it, and dusted off several decades' worth of cobwebs. "But I think I must have the wrong house. There's a little girl nearby waiting for her birthday present, so I'd better get on and get it to her." He backed away towards what he hoped was an exit. "It's been lovely meeting you and all! Bye now!"

He turned and ran. Or at least, he took a couple of very fast steps before coming up short against a collapsed wall. He heard laughter behind him.

"Nice try, not-a-girl!" squawked Chartri. "But there's no way out of this miserable place! Why do you think we've all been down here so long?"

"And here was me thinking it was because none of us had legs," said the hoard-beast.

Nadim ignored them. This was, for the most part, because the Mirror was looking straight at him.

He couldn't say how he knew that was the case. The Mirror did not, of course, possess any eyes. Nonetheless, he felt the weight of its attention on him, as if he had been wrapped within a heavy silver robe.

"Man," said the Mirror as it regarded him. "I will let you out."

Nadim looked back at it from across the room. He could see his reflection, tiny, surrounded by the silver frame like he was stepping into ornate open jaws. "I'm not sure I believe you," he said honestly.

"I am the Mirror of Truth," said the Mirror of Truth. "I do not lie. Come to me, and I will let you out."

The rest of the artefacts gave a chorus of disapproval, to the tune of 'that's not fair', and 'we're starving' and 'what sort of friend are you'.

Nadim looked around the chamber. He saw the hole he had fallen through, twice as far above him as he was tall. He saw many corners disappearing into darkness and who knew what else. He saw his leg, bloodied underneath his ripped trousers, and finally he saw the package, made out to little Roisin, clutched in his hand.

Nadim was, almost fatally, an optimist.

"Alright," he said, and stumbled towards the Mirror.

AS SOON AS NADIM STEPPED upon the ruined dais, a heavy velvet curtain descended behind him, cutting off the dismayed cries of Chartri, Dragor and the hoard-beast.

"How did you do that?" he asked, touching the fabric. It seemed to disappear up into the ceiling as far as he could see, and further still beyond that.

A disembodied smile appeared on the surface of the Mirror. "Magic," it said. "And that's just a taste of what I can offer you. Come closer, brave adventurer."

"Actually, just Nadim is fine," he said, stepping towards the Mirror. "Or Nadim the Courier, I suppose, if we're talking titles. Maybe Mr. Nadim? Um, should I call you Mrs. The Mirror of Truth?"

The Mirror went blank. Then it filled with faint images that Nadim had to squint at before he realised what they were; a dog with its head on one side, a human brow frowning, a blank signpost pointing in many directions. Images of confusion. Nadim laughed, and the images increased.

"That's very clever!" he said. "Is that the sort of magic you meant?"

The Mirror recovered, though not before its surface turned a little rosy. "What? No!" it said. "*This* is the sort of magic I meant."

And Nadim saw himself reflected in the Mirror, as one would expect, only his reflection's face was suddenly overcome with an expression of relief, and there was no blood on his reflection's leg, and no tear in his reflection's trousers. Nadim looked down at his own leg and, sure enough, it was healed.

He stumbled backwards, then flexed his leg, then did a strange little hop and jig, just to test it. "Wow," he concluded. "That really is a perfectly okay leg."

"I showed you a reflection, and the reflection came true," said the Mirror, somewhat smugly. "And I do that with your desires. Anything you wish."

Nadim paused. "So, when you said before that you were called the Mirror of Truth because you never lie- "

"Forget about that," the Mirror said. On its surface, a pair of hands made a placating gesture. "And think instead about what you want. What you want more than anything else. Riches, love, power... I can give you the throne, if you want it. I've done it before."

Nadim watched as his mirror-self walked towards a mighty silver chair, preparing to sit upon it.

"Oh, no thank you!" he said. "That thing looks pretty uncomfortable. Plus, we don't really have a monarchy here anymore."

Mirror-Nadim vanished.

"Oh," said the Mirror. "Really? What happened to Queen Miriam, second of her name, final vanquisher of the Dark Enchanter?"

Nadim bit his lip. "Ah, see, I always found the royals really boring at school, so I spent history lessons reading about the Dragon Treaties instead. Which are super interesting if you'd like a quick rundown on those-"

"I don't *care* about Dragon Treaties," the Mirror snapped, then paused. "Actually, they *do* sound fascinating, but that's not what we're here for right now."

"What are we here for right now?"

The Mirror flashed red. It rattled in its frame, dislodging a dozen errant spiderlings. "Your *greatest desire*, Nadim the Courier! The truth you most ardently seek!"

"Oh," Nadim said. "Oh, I see." He frowned. He rubbed his lip. "Yes, that is a bit more important than Dragon Treaties, isn't it?"

The Mirror sighed in relief, and once more upon its surface, a lithe, beautiful figure appeared. Its voice became waifish and whispery again.

"Then trust your desire to me, and I shall make it so."

Nadim was still pensive. "Why?" he asked, finally.

The figure in the Mirror flickered and lost its form a little. "Why what?"

"Why do you want to 'grant my greatest desire', and all that? I mean, it's very nice of you! But I seem to remember something back there about eating souls—"

"Oh *that*," the Mirror snorted. Somewhere beyond the curtain came the faint sound of several cursed artefacts arguing. "None of us actually eat souls. That's just what the stories say, you know, Chartri the wisp-torch who guides lost souls to their doom, Dragor the power-siphoning staff, the hoard-beast that offers gold then steals your spirit from out your eyeballs... all of it nonsense, of course.

"We don't 'eat' souls. We thrive off human contact, is all. I suppose it depends on who our master is. Dragor can sap the power from a hundred mages, sure, but he can also store a generation's magic for a whole community to share, if that's what they ask of him. When she lived wild in the caverns, Chartri used to trick travelers for a laugh, but she'd always send them home again after she'd had her fun. And the hoard-beast- well, I don't know exactly what he gets out of luring in greedy hands, but I don't think he'd ever killed anyone before- well. Before.

"And then there's me. But I'm sure you know that one."

"I've never actually heard the stories," Nadim admitted. "Honestly, I don't even know who the Dark Enchanter is." He hastily added, "but you all seem really into her, so I'm sure she's great!"

The Mirror filled with a sudden buzzing white light.

"*You don't—you've never—!*"

The buzzing rose to a crescendo, the already-crumbling ruins crumbling further under the strain.

"What's going on in there?!" shouted Chartri, as Dragor howled something in panic amid the sound of coins scattering.

The noise faded abruptly. The mirror turned a deep, impenetrable black. Nadim couldn't even see himself in it. There was silence for a while, and then-

"She wasn't, actually... great."

A scene appeared in the glass. An imposing woman, a little mirror glowing gold, eager, excited. The woman said something, and the mirror grew taller. The woman said something else, and the mirror became silver.

The woman built a windowless chamber. She placed the mirror inside it on a raised dais. The woman said something, and the mirror did nothing for a moment. Then it changed its reflection, became lithe, and curved, and beautiful, and not at all right. The woman brought many people to the mirror. One by one they greeted the mirror, and the woman said something, and one by one the people fell to the floor.

Now the woman sat atop a throne. But this image was different; fuzzy, unclear, as if viewed from afar or in a dream of a place you've never been. More images followed, loose, nonsensical; the woman on a ship at sea, the woman riding through a forest, the woman in valleys and mountains and deserts and tundra. And then, the mirror, clear as day, in the chamber still.

And finally, the woman in the chamber, screaming, her hands banging against the mirror's surface. The room shaking, the woman gone, the chamber collapsing. The mirror, shifting with a sigh, from its wrong human shape to a cold edifice.

Nadim let out a breath. He hadn't realised he'd been holding it.

"Okay," he said. He squeezed little Roisin's parcel between his hands. "I can't say I understood all of that."

The Mirror was carefully blank.

"But it looked... difficult. Thank you for showing me."

The Mirror was still blank. Then it said, "I wanted to see the world. That was the deal. A partnership. I made her wishes come true, and in return she would show me... anything. It didn't even have to be anything special. I would have settled for a fishpond at sunset."

A grey-blue mist like a sigh travelled across the Mirror.

"All she had to do was look in another mirror. Any kind, anywhere. Travel, look to a mirror, and I would be with her in an instant, seeing what she saw."

The Mirror quaked.

"But she never did. She never let me see anything but this room. She never let me show anything but her own reflection."

The Mirror rattled, and then was still.

"Please don't call me Mrs. The Mirror."

Nadim chewed his lip, then walked to the Mirror. He put a hand on its surface, touching his mirrored palm, looked into his own eyes, then stood to the side. "The ones like us," he said, "we can call ourselves whatever the hell we want."

The Mirror of Truth turned bright gold.

"What are you two *doing* in there?!" Chartri called, followed by an accusatory squawk from Dragor. The Mirror's golden hue took on a distinctly rose tone.

"Bonding!" Nadim called back cheerfully, just as the Mirror declared, "soul-eating!"

Nadim grinned. "You know I don't believe that now, Dr. Mirror of Truth."

"Doctor?" the Mirror asked. "I don't know what led you to think I'm a qualified surgeon-"

"Well, you fixed my leg, Doc!" Nadim laughed. "And it's a title that doesn't have a gender, if that's what you want. Or you don't have to have a title at all! But you don't have to rush into anything. Take your time. Try things out a bit, that's what I did before I settled on plain old Mister!"

"Hm," the Mirror said. "Well, I suppose I'll have a lot of time to think about it down here."

Nadim pursed his lips. "You know, I haven't told you what my *truest desire* is yet."

"Ah," the Mirror lost some of its luster. "Yes. Ahem. What is the most enduring truth of your heart, Mr. Nadim the Courier?"

Nadim lifted up the little parcel for Roisin. "To deliver this on time!" he declared.

The Mirror was silent. Its companions were not.

"What sort of person wishes to *deliver a parcel*?" the muffled voice of the hoard-beast said, while a hissing groan that was hopefully something to do with Dragor permeated the chamber.

Nadim pointed to himself. "*This* kind of person," and winked. After a second, his reflection winked back, a little exasperated.

"Very well, Nadim," the Mirror began, and on its surface, the chamber began to change.

"Wait!" Nadim said, bringing the transformation to a halt. "I forgot to add something. Are you ready?"

He struck a pose, hands on his hips, like a man who had a flair for drama and few opportunities to exercise it.

"I wish that you could see through every mirror, everywhere!"

The Mirror made an audible gulping noise.

"What?" it said. "Really?"

"Yeah," Nadim nodded. "That's my truest, deepest desire that I just thought up. Oh," he said again, "and I really *wish* and *desire* that your friends would also be able to see everything."

"Fat lot of good that is, I don't have any eyes," said the hoard-beast, but was shushed by Chartri and Dragor.

"You don't need to say 'wish' like that," said the Mirror, weakly. Its surface began to spiral into a new reflection; Nadim was there, parcel in hand, but behind him the chamber broke apart and the landscape changed, grew wooded, showed a gathering of wooden lodgings, a table loaded with fruit and sweets, and a family gathering round it.

"Yes, that looks like the right place!" Nadim said. "Thank you, I'll just-"

"Who are you talking to, son?" said a voice behind him. Nadim blinked. He was looking now not at the Mirror, but out into woodland. He turned around to see a crowd of curious faces; and among them, the farrier's cousin.

"Oh," he said. "Hello." He collected himself. "Yes, hello! I'm Nadim the Courier, I've got a parcel for someone I've been told is a very special little girl..."

The family parted to show a shy child with curly black hair done up in ribbons. He took a seat next to her and handed her the parcel with his head bowed.

"To the most esteemed Roisin on her birthday," he intoned. She took it, unwrapped it, and Nadim snorted.

Inside was a book. Its title was 'Stories for Kids: The Mirror of Truth (And Other Arcane Artefacts)'.

SOMETIME LATER, WHEN the food was all gone and the farrier's cousin had sent him back to town (with *very* detailed directions), Nadim stopped by a little fishpond. The sun hadn't quite set, and the sky was a mix of salmon pink and gold. He knelt over 'til he could see his reflection.

"Does this work as a mirror?" he said.

A second later, a green-eyed griffin, a toothy basilisk and the tarnished head of a coin glared back at him.

"You absolute fool, why didn't you just wish us out of here?!" Chartri said.

Nadim blanched. "Ah."

And the surface of the water was glowing gold, eager, excited.

Charlie Emrys

CHARLIE EMRYS IS A fantasy and sci-fi author based in the UK. Originally from a little Saxon town in England, she spent five years in Wales obtaining a first-class degree in English Literature, an MA in Creative Writing, and a smattering of dubiously pronounced Welsh. She now lives in the shadow of Glastonbury Tor, where she is frequently inspired by the local history and folklore.

When not tapping away on her laptop, Charlie enjoys making art, hiking through the nearby marshes, and spending many patient hours photographing wildlife. The natural world inspires her writing, and you will often find her reading about creatures both real and fantastical. She will also gladly talk your ear off about dinosaurs.

Old Roots, New Soil

By Sarah Lyn Eaton

Willa wandered the early morning hours before the songbirds woke. What was left of the Wernersbach's Apple Orchard was struggling to survive. Trees she remembered as green and bright red were withered and blackened. What fruit she spied was small and punky and probably only good for cider. If she was lucky, there would be enough profit to scrape through the cold months.

It might be her last winter in Pendleton.

Dried leaves crunched under her feet on a path she could have walked with her eyes closed, and often had as a child. She reached up to feel the bark of a nearby tree and where it was once smooth and silky beneath her hand; it was dry and pebbly. Willa frowned.

Her ancestors would be disappointed in her.

German hands had planted the orchard and five generations of her family had run it. There had once been four separate farms, all buttoned together by one family.

Willa was grateful that the land had been sold off by her parents into a more manageable tract. And she was grateful that they were no longer around to see what had become of the family legacy. One Wilhemina had stood on the land in 1858 and planted trees in the dirt. Another would be the one to watch the last of the trees rot in the ground.

But maybe...

She approached the edge of the orchard. She knew each farm had its own well, but the stories claimed that the original one had been boarded up and never used. It was a joke among the cousins. But her grandparents had been steadfast that it was to remain sealed. Even during the drought, they had not dared to investigate. Willa's father had argued with them, claiming the land was more important than Old World superstitions.

Her grandmother's response had been to build a vine trellis around it. In two seasons, it was completely obscured. Willa had been four then. Her memories were mostly hammers and nails and raised voices. She had always kept her distance from it, even when her grandmother slipped out at dawn to leave offerings beside it.

Willa wasn't meant to know that, but she had tailed her grandmother in the dark once.

She knew the way with her eyes closed.

HELEN WAS WAITING FOR her. Willa's stomach dropped as Helen smiled brighter than the morning light. Willa grinned tightly, tucking her short hair behind one ear. Helen winked, waving her crowbar in greeting.

"The cavalry has arrived!" Helen said cheerily.

"I appreciate it," Willa said. The vine overgrowth was denser than she had thought and was grateful for the shears she remembered to bring. "Gran's gonna be pissed."

"She's been dead for twenty years. She's over it," Helen said with a frown.

"You and I have different memories of her," Willa laughed.

"That's true." Helen eyed the contraption they were about to battle. "It all comes down?"

"It all comes down," Willa nodded.

"At least we get to share this beautiful morning," Helen said. She always said things like that. Willa blushed. Helen had lived on one of the farms which had been sold off first. She and Willa had grown up playing together through the orchard rows, chasing summer fireflies.

When Helen's parents had sold their land to a developer, Helen had been a young adult and split her time working on each of the remaining farms to make ends meet. She delivered eggs and produce to Willa from the Montgomery's Farm and helped Willa out at harvest time.

"You know," Willa choked. "If this doesn't work out. If there isn't any water in this well..."

She hung her head. Helen bit her lip and turned away. Nodding, she picked up the crowbar. Neither of them wanted to chase the end of that thought.

Sounds of splintering rendered the air. The greenery was reluctant to release its hold on the well. It was so strong that most of the aged wood broke cleanly beneath their assault. The trellis was easy. Cutting through the vines was a tedious task. Sweat formed on their brows as the sun rose over them.

It was warm for October, even in the dawn.

THEY WERE COVERED IN scratches and dirt when they were finished, but the rubbish lay to the side, exposing an old stone well. It was sealed across the top with thick wooden boards and long iron nails. The removal of the vines revealed a family history previously unknown to Willa.

All around the base of the stone wall were old pieces of crockery, dirty and chipped, with dried remnants of offerings long gone caked in the bottoms. They were littered with discarded snake sheds and the skeletons of small rodents.

"Shit," Willa said with a whistle. There were dozens of small jars and bowls. Her grandmother was obviously not the first one to leave them. Maybe she'd learned it from her own grandmother.

"Your ancestors weren't kidding around," Helen frowned. "Maybe the well was poisoned?"

Willa sighed. Helen was probably right. No one went to such great lengths to keep people out without a reason. "They probably didn't want any of the kids falling in," she said. "This well is closest to the house."

"That tracks," Helen nodded. "Is it too early for a beer?"

"We haven't had breakfast yet," Willa laughed.

"How do we break into the vault?"

"More elbow grease."

"Do we want to clean up the pottery first?"

Willa looked around. She spied an empty apple box under a nearby tree as the wind picked up. The leaves on the trees flipped upside-down and Willa's stomach was uneasy. When was the last time hands had touched the small offerings?

"No," she said. "Let's wait to see if the well is even any good before we disturb what the dead made."

"When you put it that way, I am so less interested in touching them." Helen's voice was sober. Willa nodded in kind.

"Understood," she said. The sun beat down on them as they wrested the long nails from where they had been driven deep into the mortar between the stone. She pulled the last nail out with a deep exhalation. It was as if they had been hammered in while the mortar was still wet.

Helen glanced at her watch.

"All right?" Willa asked breathlessly.

"We missed breakfast. My fuel cells are about two percent. I think we should break for lunch."

"We did the hard part already," Willa chuckled. But her arms felt a little wobbly. "We're almost there."

"Then how about I go scrounge up some food and bring it back?"

Willa nodded.

"Are we feeling lucky?" Helen asked with a twinkle. Her curly hair blew around her eyes. "Do I bring us celebratory beers?"

Willa's words escaped before she heard them. "Bring one for the well, too. It's been a while since anyone has shown it gratitude." Willa chuckled and shrugged. "That's something I heard Gran say to my dad once."

"You got it, boss," Helen said, disappearing quickly through the thinning orchard trees.

THE THICKEST AND OLDEST tree stood beside the well, the first that Wilhemina Wernersbach had planted in their new soil. Family stories said the original apple tree had been brought over from their homeland in Germany, near the Black Forest. The same forest made famous through Grimm's fairy tales.

It was a nice story. The curious part of it for Willa was that the tree was still producing the best fruit, even as the other trees waned.

She took her work gloves off and poked at the boards covering the well. They were roughly hewn planks from an old mill. The undersides seemed punkish and were buckling slightly. Willa took that as a sign of moisture beneath them. She placed her hands on the well, one on the wood and another on the stone. She thought she tasted water in her mouth.

Please, she whispered. She needed no other words. She prayed as if she believed in its magic. *Gran did.*

Gran had believed in her.

She pushed at one of the boards, which also seemed to have been laid down atop fresh mortar. With a grunt, Willa put all of her one-hundred and seventy pounds into the push and the board gave with a groan of its own. Once freed, it was easy to move.

"Shit!" Willa exclaimed, shaking her hand. A splinter had scraped across her palm and blood welled up along its edge.

Willa recoiled at the stench that assaulted her when the wood was pulled away. It wasn't an altogether unpleasant smell, she thought, though her skin crawled at the idea that anyone could adapt to such an odor.

As the offending air dissipated, cool moisture wafted up from the well, but it was all dark inside. The dark was deep. Willa leaned over with the flashlight and grimaced as a trickle of blood ran down her palm. She shook it off and wiped it on her pants. There it was, the water. It was higher up in the chamber than she'd expected. She frowned. There were so many lean years. Her grandparents had struggled so much...

Why had they never tapped this well?

She wept with joy. Maybe she wouldn't be the last Wernersbach to live on the Pendleton soil.

The undisturbed surface of the water was a mirror. She saw herself holding the light over the darkness. As she watched, other faces wore her skin. Five generations of her family, she thought. A drop of blood slipped off the heel of her hand.

It fell, breaking the surface tension of the well water, rippling out, obscuring the past. The wind whipped up.

"STORM'S COMING," HELEN said, reappearing with two sandwiches and three cold beers. "I take it from your face that there's water?"

"There's water," Willa said, grinning with unexpected relief. Helen grinned in return. Willa took the third beer and uncapped it, setting it at the base of the old tree.

"Do apple nymphs drink beer?" Helen asked. Willa shrugged.

"Trees have dryads," she said.

Helen rolled her eyes. "Do apple trees have dryads?"

"Gran always talked about the birch dryads. I don't know about the apple trees. Can't hurt, right?"

"Fair enough." Helen leaned back against the well wall. Her voice dipped intimate and low. "Guess this means I'll be around a while longer," she said. Willa could feel the warmth of her nearness.

She nodded. "Guess it does."

Willa smiled. The sun was shining down on the earth she stood on, that she'd been born on. There was water in the well. At least part of the orchard could still be saved. It was a glorious day.

WILLA WOKE WITH DREAMS of being tapped into the new well by dusk. She dressed hurriedly and grabbed a slice of toast before heading out the door. She stopped dead in her tracks, shaking her head.

Surely, I am still asleep.

Every tree in the orchard stood upright, silver branches covered in impossibly bright green leaves, thick branches laden with ripe and raucous red apples.

Willa approached the nearest tree. Her hand ran along its bark, smooth as silk. She gasped. Her hand shook as she reached for an apple. It pulled easily from the branch. Its fruit was so fragrant she felt light-headed. She bit into it, the juice running down her chin before she could stop it.

It was the most delicious apple she had ever eaten from the orchard.

Willa didn't understand. She glanced up the hill at the exposed well. She shook her hand. It couldn't be. They hadn't connected it to the orchard yet.

"Hell's bells," Helen said behind her, still buttoning her flannel. "Am I dreaming?"

"If you are, I am." Willa swallowed hard.

"Then I believe we are both dreams walking," Helen whispered.

Willa nodded. She understood. It was a miracle.

She also saw that every apple was ripe on the trees. She could already smell the rot waiting to slip in. And there were a lot of trees for two people.

"WILLA," THE YOUNG COLLEGE kid said. "That's an odd name." His name was Bennett. Willa thought it equally odd, but as if conjured by magic, he had stepped into the orchard that afternoon, looking for summer work.

"It's an old one. It wasn't odd for Germany in the 1800s, I'm guessing," Willa shrugged. "I was named after my great-great-great-great grandmother, who arrived at Ellis Island in 1858 with her three sons in tow."

"No husband?"

Willa rolled her eyes.

"I'm sure she had one at some point."

"Ellis Island I get," Bennett said, dropping some apples into his sling bag. "But Pendleton, NY? It's kind of in the middle of nowhere."

"Your migration found you at my roadside today," Willa laughed with a shrug. "Her brother was here already. She bought a parcel of land next to him. Her oldest son bought a parcel next to her for his young family. Over the next five years, she bought up another tract and gave it to her second oldest. They planted apples on every open inch. The youngest inherited her parcel. In their hey-day the Wernersbachs were responsible for hiring the largest number of summer migrant workers in the county."

He looked around appreciatively. "I can see that. I'm surprised you don't have more workers."

Willa snorted. "You should have been here yesterday."

"Why's that?"

She shrugged. "It was looking like a hard year." Helen collected apples a few rows over. Willa chewed on the inside of her cheek. The kid had a good point. They needed more hands or the apples would go soft before she could get them to market.

I did wish for this bounty, she thought.

THEY STOPPED FOR DINNER. Her arms and back were sore and aching. Even still, she prepared the Dutch baby just as she had with her Gran. The batter sat in a bowl beside her and she sauteed the fresh apples up with cinnamon and brown sugar in an iron skillet. When they were soft enough, she poured the batter over them and put the whole pan in the oven to bake.

Even though her arms ached, the familiar ritual was comforting.

"You are in for a treat," Helen told Bennett as they set the table.

"That'll take about a half-hour. Helen, think we could borrow a few hands from the Montgomery's?" Willa asked. Helen nodded.

"If there's money coming to them on the other side of selling the harvest, they'll be fighting over who gets to come."

"Good." Willa smiled in relief. She should be grateful for the bounty, as mystical as it seemed. She should be grateful for Helen's extended stay. But her stress over the thought of losing something she hadn't anticipated having was oppressive.

The rocking chair in the corner began to move in the wind coming through the open door. Willa poured out a cup of tea and set it beside the chair. Helen made a sound behind her.

"That's for your Gran, isn't it?"

"Yes."

"Funny," she said. "It's similar to your Gran leaving bowls of whatever at the well, isn't it?"

Willa grinned crookedly at Helen. "I guess it is."

"I think it's sweet."

Bennett cleared his throat. "I'm going to go harvest a bit more." He cleared his throat again, carrying out a glass of water. "For about twenty minutes. So, I won't be here. In the kitchen. I won't be here at all. I'll be outside."

Helen giggled as he walked out of the room. "What do you think he was implying?"

Willa was hyper-aware of Helen's hand, brushing along the birch countertop, coming closer to where she stood. She held her breath. She leaned in for a kiss—

Outside, glass shattered.

Willa ran for the door. Bennett stood on the porch, shaking his head. The water glass was strewn in shards at his feet. All the apple bins throughout the orchard were overflowing with bright red fruit. The entire harvest was finished.

"I don't believe it," Bennett said.

"This isn't possible," Willa said.

"If you're dreaming, we all are," Helen whispered. "What was in that well? Gas?"

"I wasn't here for that," Bennett said quietly.

"Oh," Helen said. "What do we do now?"

"We go to market before we wake up," Willa replied. *We save my farm.*

WILLA'S HEART WAS FULL. She was far from out of the hole, but she could see a way out and it was enough. When she kissed Helen that night, she poured her gratitude for whatever curse had broken on her property into it. She poured all of her memories of happy childhoods wearing daisy wreaths on her head and dancing in circles to celebrate the sun into the arms of her oldest friend and deepest love. And when she fell into sleep, her heart was so full, she did not dream.

SOMETHING MOVED IN the house. It would be Bennett, Willa thought, opening her eyes in the dark. But she didn't hear the expected sounds of feet moving to the bathroom or kitchen. Instead, she heard the front door slam closed.

Helen slept soundly as Willa slid her nightshirt and her slippers on. She passed the guest room and cracked the door open slightly. Willa's heart skipped.

Bennett was sleeping in his bed.

Willa quickened her pace through the house. The rocking chair in the kitchen corner moved with the breeze coming in through the open door. Willa grabbed it before it could slam closed again.

Why is it open at all?

Willa stepped out onto the porch. A white figure slipped into the trees.

"Hey!" Willa exclaimed, chasing after it. It ran faster up the hill.

I knew it wasn't magic, Willa thought. She knew she chased after her mysterious benefactor. She ran faster down the path she could have run blind.

"I just want to thank you!" she yelled into the dark. She stumbled into the clearing by the well, out of breath.

A pale being launched itself across the glade at her. She tripped backwards, falling onto her back end. The creature licked at the cut on her hand with a grunt. Willa recoiled from its skin, giving off the same odor she smelled inside the well.

"Oath-breaker," it croaked out, growling at her. "Thank us. Now."

"WHAT DID YOU CALL ME?" Willa asked as she cringed. The being sneered. Its skin was soft in a sallow way, like a thing that hadn't seen the sun in decades.

Or a century.

"I smell like home. This is not home." It approached the oldest tree and stroked the bark. "This is of home."

"What did you call me?" Willa repeated.

"Oath-breaker," the thing said, staring at the wooden boards on the ground. It picked up a long iron nail and licked the length of it, nodding at her.

"Were you inside the well?" she asked.

The only answer it gave was a grin full of sharp teeth, more teeth than belonged in a mouth. Its eyes were not eyes. They were black voids, like dark galaxies in motion. It was unsettling.

Willa gagged on the stench.

"We help. Now you pay."

"Pay how?" Willa asked. The thing frowned, tilting its head.

"You don't pay," it hissed, "we take." It turned its head dramatically towards the house.

Willa shook her head. "No, please! I want to pay. I just don't understand what you want."

"Wilhemina Wernersbach made us a promise. That this land was us, too. The first water was ours."

"And I broke it," Willa said. The thing nodded. Her skin was creeping.

"You used blood magic to open the door. And we helped. And now you won't pay. So, we take." It inched towards the house. Willa's heart thundered.

What have I done?

"So, you helped Wilhemina, too?"

"Of course," the being frowned. "You know nothing."

"That's true."

"Ignorance does not release you."

"I'm understanding that."

The thing crawled towards the nearest apple bin, where fruit spilled over onto the ground. It hissed gleefully and put a hand on the wood. Willa watched in horror as the apples began to brown and rot until the scent of decay was so cloying in the air she started to cough.

"What are you?" she asked.

"Wilhemina had four sons."

"No," Willa frowned. "She had three."

"She crossed the ocean with four. Four sons. Four trees. All died but one. Did not like this land. I do not like this land. It takes from us to make things grow."

Horror blossomed in Willa's belly.

"Are you... are you Wilhemina's fourth son?"

The thing cackled madly, so loud that the branches around them shook with equal measure. "No," it said, bouncing around the clearing. It leapt atop the well wall and slunk towards her along the edge. "I am the thing that followed them over."

"And what did you require for payment?"

The thing licked its lips. "Life for life." It was waiting for her.

Willa swallowed. "I am the last Wernersbach here."

The thing jumped down beside her. It ran a hand down her leg. It was panting. Willa dragged herself backwards.

Please let me be sleeping soundly in bed beside Helen. But the hand stroking her was very real. Her heart rate quickened. Its teeth gnashed together.

A voice drifted up through the dark orchard.

"Willa?"

The thing's head whipped around towards the sound. It ran, dragging Willa by the thigh behind it. Willa's head hit stone and her vision blurred.

THE ROCKING CHAIR MOVED in the corner. Willa's Gran sat in it, sipping her tea. She couldn't see Willa, who was in her hiding place beside the coal bin. Gran sat until the house was quiet. Then she made her way out into the night.

Willa was close behind.

Gran carried a small bowl with her. Willa could see the old woman was following her own specter, of an old woman carrying a small bowl. And that woman followed another ghost, a plump young woman with a small jar. And she followed an old woman in a long nightgown.

Even from a distance Willa could hear the ghosts crying.

When they entered the clearing, they all walked, not to the well, but to the oldest tree in the orchard. One by one, they stepped into each other, layering their generations of offerings into one. It evaporated into ether as Gran stepped into that space. Her lips were moving, but Willa could not hear them.

It was not the well. It was the tree. The trees.

The orchard.

A SCREAM PIERCED THE air as Willa opened her eyes. The trees shook their branches in distress. She stood shakily, tottering over to the first planted. She stepped up to it, picking up the beer from earlier and upended it along the roots.

"I honor you," she spat the words out. "I honor you as one of your own. Help me. Help us!"

All the trees lifted their heads and arms. They all turned to Willa. She stepped backwards, clutching the bottle in her hand.

"*Close the door.*"

Willa heard Helen scream. Bennett yelled. Her heart thundered. She understood. She stepped to the edge of the wall and broke the bottle against the stone. Cutting her palm open, she shook her blood down into the well. Droplets broke the surface tension of the mirror.

Something moved below.

The thing galloped into the clearing at her with a rending shriek. Willa spied blood on its mouth and she shivered. She closed her eyes. As it lunged for her, she grabbed it first and flipped it over her head, using her body weight to complete the arc.

Willa Wernersbach fell into the darkness. Her feet slipped into nothing. The thing scrambled up her thighs, struggling for purchase. Willa inhaled well water.

Life for life.

WILLA CHOKED OUT LIQUID against the sounds of banging metal on stone. She blinked furiously. Helen was directing Bennett loudly. They were both hammering the old wooden boards back into the wall. Helen's arm was red with blood.

"Helen?" Willa croaked.

"You said close the door!" Helen yelled. "I hope this is what you meant. You better not be dying on me over there!"

Willa knew the door was already closed. Wilhemina Wernersbach had opened it once with the blood of her son. Maybe he had died of starvation or dehydration. Maybe she had taken his life in a moment of desperation. Wernersbach blood had opened a way for their land wights to find purchase in the new world. Wernersbach blood had closed the way to the Old Ones.

She could see a future where Helen worked in the kitchen, preparing a meal for them. Willa could feel her feet on the grass as she carried a small bowl of apple slices and honey and milk through the orchard, leaving it for the spirits of the land.

Whatever land their feet found them standing on.

Sarah Lyn Eaton

SARAH LYN EATON IS a queer pagan writer and burn survivor. She is a lifelong Star Wars geek who spends her free time rock hunting, or venturing into the woods with her camera. Her stories have been published in the anthologies *Brave New Worlds, Upon a Twice Time, Unburied: A Collection of Queer Dark Fiction, Of Fae and Fate: Lesser Known Fairy Tales Retold, On Fire,* and *Dystopia Utopia*. In 2021, Sarah Lyn was awarded The Speculative Literature Foundation's Working Class Writer Grant.

Hell's Angel

By Victory Witherkeigh

"You are finally ready to graduate from hell."

It's the only thing written on Callisto's birthday card, not even a name signed at the end. She wanted to tell herself the card was a congratulatory message. But it didn't feel congratulatory. As much as she knew this day was coming, the butterflies in her stomach persisted night after night.

I guess even the heir to the throne of the dead gets nervous too, she thought as she tried to soothe her stomach, holding the card.

Callisto had heard the stories of her parents' love her entire life. Or, instead, she had listened to the legends and myths borne from their desire over the centuries. It made some sense. Her father, Hades, would tell her as a little girl, "It's not every day that the god of death finds love, much less a lover who accepts what comes with the title. Your mother is an exceptional being..." he'd tell her wistfully each night he tucked her into bed.

For the longest time, Callisto asked her father to tell her the various stories of her parents' first meeting, giggling at the variations. While their relationship was unique with her mother tending the mortal realms for months at a time each year, that she was a helpless nymph dragged to the belly of a beastly grave made Callisto giggle without end.

"Hrmp... it's not funny, Hades!" Her mother would scoff when she was there to tuck in their daughter with him. "You never get underestimated! They all bow down to Death... Spring is just something they take for granted..."

"Now, darling," he'd reply, kissing her hand as their daughter closed her eyes, "We both know that you are the formidable one between the two of us. Let them have their stories. We know the truth..."

It was that truth of their love that kept them going as a couple, despite the separation. Hades would tell Callisto it was her mother's love that gave him the strength to try for a child at all, as he had long believed that life could not come from the god of death. Despite the years of trial and error, miscarriages, and heartache for both himself and Persephone, the sheer joy of their discovery of Callisto's conception was enough to throw the first party in Tartarus within a millennium. They considered her their miracle child, a symbol of the circle of life into death and back again. It was enough of a miracle Zeus and Poseidon reconciled with their brother, not wanting to miss out on the only child born to the family in hundreds of years.

Callisto had heard the mortal tales of her aunts and uncles as a child. The incestuous stories of women taken against their will by her uncles made her face crinkle and her cheeks red.

How could they have gotten the stories so wrong? she thought, playing with the little toys they'd leave her.

It wasn't until she was older that she learned how cut off her parents were from most of her family. Time in the dead's land was obsolete, and communication outside the realm to the mortal world was almost unheard of. Persephone would bring back news when she came back from her duties in fulfilling Spring, but considering the other three seasons had the family isolated, there were vast periods without the family noticing. Hades was the only one aware when mortals lost their faith and belief in his family. He watched as the myths grew more elaborate and intense. He stood by his brothers and sisters as each of them passed on, becoming his subjects as they moved to the Elysian Fields of Heaven or the Hell of Tartarus. Persephone was the one who noted that they would one day need to pass on. Both Callisto's parents had brought her up, knowing that she would one day take her father's place on the throne.

Immortality was just one more of the elaborate myths that had spread about her relatives over the years. They were blessed with certain powers attributed to the natural world, but even they could not live forever. Their magic gave each of them their own avenues for extending their already long lives. Her cousin Ares used the blood harvested during battles to regenerate his body to its pristine form. Her other cousin Aphrodite would use the fluids of her sexual conquests to rebuild and extend her beauty and grace. Aunt Hera feasted off the placenta of the children brought forth from the marriages and families she helped foster. Hades told his daughter that his life tied to the number of souls reaching the underworld and the absence of time. Her mother would age more quickly because of her interactions with the mortal realm tied with the thriving of life on the planet.

"One day, my dear," he said during her first years of schooling in Latin, "Your mother believes that there will come a day when Gaia dies off with the advances of humanity. The cycle of pollution and waste is getting stronger... as your mother's time ends, I believe that will be an agreeable time to transfer the throne to you..."

"But... where will you go?" she begged with tears in her eyes, "What will happen to me?"

"You will be the Queen of the Underworld, my dear. You have the best of your mother and myself - a balance of life that lets you walk in the sun, and the empathy needed for death. I have every faith in the world that you'll be a magnificent leader..."

"I don't want to be alone! I don't want you and mom to die off away from me! Don't leave me behind!"

Hades held his daughter in his arms as she cried relentlessly for weeks, trying to soothe her, telling her it would be okay. But he also knew the heartache she would face. How many eons had passed before he met Persephone? How many lonely millennia passed as he watched from the sidelines as the rest of his family found love and friendships?

As Callisto grew older, her mother and father divided up her studies into shifts within his realm. Persephone showed her the mortal realm early as a child, wanting to explain the unexplainable concepts when she was the most open - concepts like hope, imagination, magic.

"Humans have an interesting coping mechanism for their reality," she'd tell Callisto, "They look at my work with the coming of Spring, the sign that life can begin again and run with it... Some have this inexplicable understanding that if they can harness their will enough, they can push through the impossible and make things happen..."

"But mom," Callisto would say, "They waste so many things. They hurt your trees and plants... isn't that wrong?"

"It depends on who you ask, my dear...They are not great at recognizing the patterns in their mistakes. They don't see the enormous picture like your father and you..."

In the mortal realm, Callisto learned what it meant to have your blood pumping through your veins as a horse raced through the forest. Her cousin Artemis taught her the skill of the hunt, the grace of using a blade. Ares supervised her lessons with the sword and the shield before showing her man's newest inventions with gunpowder and automation. He'd goad her into striking harder, throwing her weight into a kill.

"You'll learn soon enough, Callisto," Ares said. "There is no thrill like the sensation of striking your palm through someone's chest, grabbing their beating heart and squeezing slowly..."

Hades furrowed his brow in those lessons, reminding her cousin that death was no laughing matter, but Callisto understood what Ares meant. Her father's jurisdiction only came after death's final blow, not in the passing of life. She knew his view was much more detached than her cousins - who was there for the bloodiest method mortals saw their lives end. At ten, Callisto's learning took a fresh turn, exploring the heavenly dimensions.

"Your mother and I agreed that you'll study in the heavenly realms from here until fourteen..." Hades casually mentioned over dinner on her tenth birthday. "Once you turn fourteen, you'll transfer for the next four years to the hellish ones."

"Are you telling me I'll be in hell for high school?" asked Callisto.

Persephone could only smirk at her husband during that dinner as he blushed, indignant that his child was growing so modern. While they had taught her the ancient languages of the civilizations long forgotten, Callisto spoke with a modern slang of an American child. She enjoyed television and cruising the malls from time to time. It was almost as if she saw people as dolls to play with instead of full-fledged beings. Still, they pressed forward with her study in the heavenly realms, much to Callisto's annoyance.

Callisto couldn't vocalize this to anyone, but her years of study in the heavenly realms were some of the most boring. Every day, the joy and the peace floating through the universe numbed her out. She didn't understand why she didn't enjoy it, but the studies of meditation or the viewing of time as a kaleidoscope only dragged on and on. The music was beautiful, but she found that the feeling of dread growing in the pit of her stomach sped up.

Persephone moved slower each time she visited her child. Callisto would notice the traces of black along the hem of her clothes, the hacking coughs when her mother thought no one was looking. She'd catch her mother cycle between growing violently ill, passing out and vomiting, incoherent with poisons, or burning with literal flames in her hair. In the dark of night, she'd hear her cousins or father whisper of the growing decay humanity was producing, the worry in their voices as it took Persephone longer and longer to recover. Some seasons, Persephone would only go a few weeks before returning to the underworld, exclaiming that Apollo was oozing with longer and longer rides on his chariot.

"Dad," Callisto whispered the night before her fourteenth birthday, finding him in their kitchen, eating alone, "Can I talk to you?"

"Sure thing, darling. What are you doing up so late? You have a big day tomorrow..."

"Why... why do you spend so much time... I mean, why do you rule from the house? I mean, you have the Elysium or the Isles of the Blessed? Why is our house in the middle, with the river and...?"

Hades could see the tears forming in her eyes, pleading that he answers honestly.

"My time as the king has been about balance, Callisto. When I first came to this kingdom, it was so overwhelming... the Styx, Cerberus, Tartarus... the flow of souls... I thought I'd drown in all of it... so I wanted to be in the most helpful location - the eye of the hurricane..."

Callisto sniffed and nodded, even though she wasn't sure she understood.

"I'm scared, Dad..." she breathed out softly, "I'm scared for mom... for you... I want to stop it... I want to help, but I'm useless."

"Shhh... No... no honey, you're not..."

"Daddy... I... want to hurt them... I want them to pay for what they've done to mom... to you..."

He wrapped his arms around his daughter, unsure of what to say in response to that statement. His "little girl" was no longer a child, and as a ruler, he could not ignore the fear in his gut at those words. Hades had spent eons discussing the need for impartiality on the throne of the dead, the understanding of the power in judging and sentencing those souls who came before him. But his daughter was slowly watching her mother suffer, rotting away from the actions those very souls performed without regard.

"I know it's easy to say that, my dear. Especially when you see the peace and rewards waiting in our kingdom... but you must have faith in me and your mother. We have set up our system for a reason... you remember why I must..."

"Stay impartial for the judgment..." she muttered to finish his sentence. "I know you say that, Dad. But I'm not you. And I'm not Mom. I don't... what if I can't do this like you guys?"

"You still have time, love... I'm not going anywhere yet..."

From the first day in the hellish realms, Callisto could no longer complain about the endless boredom overcoming her days. Getting to the various instructors alone proved harrowing. Hades almost stepped in as the grip of tormented souls drowning in the boiling rivers of blood grabbed and clawed at her ankles. Callisto's heart hammered in her chest, and she fought back, fighting the slight warmth in her belly, forming as the rage she'd been carrying for her mother finally had an outlet to go. Her first year, she learned the overview and tiered systems of the punishments according to her father's sentencing. He took a more hands-on approach as he instructed her through sentencing and the weave of transport between the levels of hell.

Unlike the heavenly realms, there was no flow of travel back and forth between souls as they judged them. They all walked past some more unusual punishments like Sisyphus or Paris and Helena to let what little mental facilities left imagine the worst. In year two, Callisto learned the techniques of Sadism and watching for the Masochistic. She was the most proficient with the needles and the daggers her father found. She had the most trouble when it involved their dogs, Cerberus, and his pups.

"The pups are so young, dad, they don't deserve the scratches and the clawing..." she'd whisper to her father.

"They have to learn the commands, Callisto. Even Cerberus won't live forever... and a guard dog has always been with our family."

"I just think they might like a better snack... like a real steak, or a bone... not just gnashing at the dead..."

"Well, at least we know there's some mercy in you," he replied with his eyebrow raised.

By year three, they allowed Callisto to the lowest levels - the hellish punishments from the very fears of the damned. Some souls were so rotten, so vile that their sentences came from their subconscious rather than her father's. It seemed the most appropriate that only the most depraved could come up with something that would punish themselves. Callisto would have "retreats" into these hells, needing to show the strength and fortitude of her own mind as she entered the hellscapes designed by the serial killers, dictators, etc. They forced her to endure the sensation of her nerves severing as her skin peeled slowly away and flayed on a barbeque for dinner. Callisto even aided a wife in constructing a sex toy from her husband's ashes to show he could never leave her, left her after she hacked him piece by piece for trying. Those trials left her shivering on the shower floor that year.

Callisto folded the birthday card before pulling out the small hidden panel in her headboard. It contained all the mementos from her mother. Persephone now resigned to bedrest most of the year as Hades and Callisto took on caring for her. She would lie like a vegetable until the Springtime came closer. It had been years since Callisto could remember what it felt like to hug her mom, smell her shampoo of lotus flowers, and Jasmine wafting through the hallways. This card was one of the last she knew her mother had written out before the pollution and sickness took hold completely, leaving them for Hades to give to Callisto for every holiday and birthday she'd missed.

"Callisto!" yelled Hades, "Time for the Birthday girl to be getting ready!! Your graduation won't be starting without you!"

"I'm up, Dad!"

Callisto looked down at the photos of her and her parents. The smiles on their faces over the eons with her family. As much as eighteen on earth seems so young, Callisto knew she was over two thousand years old now, if they regarded time at all. She had done her duty, fulfilled all the lessons and tests her father and her uncles put forth for the last four years. Callisto knew that day in the kitchen with Hades that he had feared her for the first time. It was a chilling moment, the moment a child realizes they can scare their parents, that they have the power to frighten the ones they love. She knew her father, and as much as she loved the man, she also knew she wasn't him. Her deepest secret, the thoughts she kept to herself all these years as she played the role of the future Queen, pushed her to stay sane in the worst hellscapes. Hades had raised his daughter to be reliable, formidable, and magnificent. Callisto was that, and more, but she had inherited one trait from her cousin she'd hidden all these years - her bloodlust.

For all the torture, rot, and punishment hell had, Callisto could feel in her bones the singing gratification of the blood surrounding her. There was no hell greater for her than watching her mother become a shell of herself, losing her life slowly to the animals traipsing around above. After all these years, all this time waiting, the nerves and butterflies weren't about if she'd fail. Callisto knew there would be no room for failure as a ruler. Her kingdom, her family, had made enough sacrifices to get her here. This was her chance.

I promise, Mom... I promise I'll bring you back...

I don't care what it takes.

I'll kill them all to bring you back... I'll make them pay.

Victory Witherkeigh

VICTORY WITHERKEIGH is a female Filipino author originally from Los Angeles, CA, currently living in the Las Vegas area. Victory was a finalist for Wingless Dreamer's 2020 Overcoming Fear Short Story award and a 2021 winner of the Two Sisters Writing and Publishing Short Story Contest. She has print publications in the horror anthologies Supernatural *Drabbles of Dread* through Macabre Ladies Publishing, *Bodies Full of Burning* through Sliced Up Press, and *In Filth It Shall Be Found* through OutCast Press. Her first novel, set to debut with Cinnabar Moth Publishing (date TBA), has been a finalist for Killer Nashville's 2020 Claymore Award, a 2020 Cinnamon Press Literature Award Honoree, and long-listed in the 2021 Voyage Y.A. Book Pitch Contest.

The Story Witch

By Kaye Lynne Booth

Deep in the darkest part of the forest, lived a witch named Tabitha, who spun stories, as well as spells. They called her Tiny Tabby, when they thought about her at all, because she was so small that she lived inside a large toadstool which grew from the rich, dark earth at the base of the oldest Sequoia tree. Tabitha chose to make her home there, far away from the rest of the world, where she could be left in peace to write stories and weave spells.

The world had not been kind to the wee witch, who was small enough to need to dodge between feet on the busy city streets to avoid being stomped by bustling people in too much of a hurry to even notice that she was there. And so, she had retreated to the depths of the forest, where the birds and beasts of the forest seldom ventured, and the sun rarely touched the pine needles layering the forest floor. While it was true that it was dark and musty, she was seldom disturbed from her writing. After a field mouse who had been chased by fox ran up her toadstool one day and perched in the eaves of the cap, nibbling at the edges in an attempt to make a meal of her cozy little home, she conjured a cat to chase off any unknowing creatures who might wander this far in.

Most days went by with Tabitha writing her stories undisturbed, taking time out only to eat and feed the cat, who spent most of its time curled up in her kitty bed by the fireplace. Tabitha had given it food and named it Puss, and because mice seldom ventured this deeply into the forest, Puss had become somewhat of a lazy cat, growing plump on rabbit stew made from the catch of Tabitha's snares, which were always full, due to the enchantments she placed upon them.

Most of Tabitha's magic was woven into her stories, which were wonderful tales of adventure and daring. Day after day, her enchanted keyboard typed out her words as she paced from one side of the toadstool to the other, dictating the stories that came into her head. One after another she stacked the completed stories in a box on the corner of her desk, until eventually, the stack reached the ceiling and overflowed into a new stack on the floor, and then another and another, until there was only a small space left around her desk and she had to clear a path to the fireplace so she could keep the fire ablaze to hold the darkness at bay and keep her little toadstool warm. Finally, she was forced to stop pacing and dictating, as there was no room left in which to stack her pages. Something had to be done. If Tabitha wanted to continue writing, (and she did, writing stories was her favorite thing to do), then she had to find a way to clear out the old and share them with the bigger world in order to make room for the new. She knew just the spell that would accomplish the task for her.

So, Tabitha set out into the forest to gather up the ingredients that she would need for that particular spell: a pinch of wolfsbane; seven caps of an unusually rare mushroom only found in the darkest patches of the forest where sunlight could not penetrate the canopy of the trees; a handful of hog's warts, which are not at all easy to get because wild hogs are slippery and not likely to give their warts up without a valent fight; and the whiskers of an enormous catfish which lived deep down on the very bottom of the lake. She had to wrestle him into submission, since catfish are rather fond of their whiskers, and once plucked, they do not grow back.

Now most of these ingredients were quite difficult to obtain, which is as it should be, since magic should never be easy. If spells were simple to cast, everyone would be conjuring. No casting spells is an art, and they require both skill and talent, like any other creative endeavor, along with a certain amount of acquired knowledge. But the last step in this particular spell was the hardest, calling for all the ingredients to be mixed together and heated to a boil with the breath of a dragon.

Tabitha did know of a dragon, Zarg, who lived in a cave, deep in the heart of the mountain. She wasn't on good terms with him after she'd distracted him with a mock attack on his cave long enough for her to snatch a few dragon scales from the floor of his lair where he'd shed them. That wouldn't make her task any easier. Zarg was a smart dragon who didn't take kindly to being made to look a fool. He wasn't likely to have forgotten Tabitha's trickery. Never-the-less, once she'd gathered together all the ingredients she needed, she set off toward the mountain, drawing the fireproof cloak that her grandmother had made for her around her tight to ward of the chill that the deep shade of the forest brought with it.

As she made her way through the darkest part of the forest, the fireflies she'd summoned lighting the way, it was her good fortune to come across a rabbit which had been lost within the forest depths for so long that it hopped around blindly, with no way to find food or protect itself from forest predators, of which Tabitha was only one of many.

Everyone knew the way to a dragon's heart was through his stomach, so Tabitha built a fire and cooked up a lovely rabbit stew to offer up in apology for deceiving him. There was no guarantee that it would work, but Tabitha believed her chances were good, so she took extra time to search out the most delicious ingredients available to flavor her stew just right. When the stew was done, she continued on her way to Zarg's cave, where she hoped she could convince the big flying lizard to cook up her spell with his breath.

When she reached the cave entrance, she pulled the hood of her fireproof cloak up over her head and clasped it tightly in her fist at her throat before crossing the threshold, with her fireflies leading the way. She made her way through the winding passages of the cave, following them down into the depths of the mountain, where she knew Zarg lay curled around his precious gold. She had never understood what fascination dragons had with gold. After all, they couldn't spend it. Yet, every dragon she had ever heard of guarded a pile of it, treating it as their most prized possession, and Zarg was no exception.

The day she'd swiped the dragon scales, she'd seen Zarg's treasure mound, piled so high that it almost touched the ceiling of the cavern. She'd taken care to gather the scales along the outer cavern walls, keeping a respectful distance between herself and Zarg's precious gold. That's the only thing that saved her from his scorching breath, but even so, a dragon isn't likely to forgive, or to forget.

The nearer she came to his lair, the more doubt crept into her mind. *Would a simple rabbit stew really be enough to persuade the beast to help her?* She began to think that maybe this hadn't been such a good idea after all. Before she could change her mind and turn around, she rounded a corner in the tunnel and stepped into the gigantic cavern, where the huge green lizard sprawled across the top of the enormous pile of gold and silver, and gems galore, his wings spread out with their tips touching the ground on each side. It was as if Zarg were trying to cover the whole mountain of sparkly things in his loving embrace, and Tabitha detected a slight upturn to his black, rubbery lips as each rumbling snore erupted from them; a sure sign of sleeping easy and having pleasant dreams. Although she'd only had that one other encounter with Zarg, she was pretty sure waking a fire-breathing dragon from a dream he was obviously enjoying would be a very bad idea. All she could do was to pull up a rock at the edge of the cavern—as close to the entry tunnel as she could manage in case of the need for a quick get-away—and wait for the beast to awaken.

As Tabitha sat on her rock, waiting for the dragon to awaken, it occurred to her if she could find a pleasant way to wake the dragon, he might not be too irritated, and she thought she knew just how to do it. She pulled the pot of rabbit stew out from inside her fireproof cowl—there's a lot more room within a witch's cowl than one might think—and she built a fire on top of a discarded dragon scale she found on the cavern floor. Now one might not think it smart to build a fire in a cave deep inside a mountain, but Tabitha figured it would be safe, as there had to be a hole in the cathedralic ceiling where the smoke from the dragon's breath could escape.

Before long, the stew was bubbling in the cauldron, and the aroma of rabbit cooking wafted up from within. Tabitha watched Zarg quite closely. She held her breath when she saw one of his nostrils twitch until his snoring resumed. A few minutes later, he rolled onto his back, breathing in a deep breath with both nostrils, and then, all at once, the dragon's eyes flew open wide.

"Something smells delicious," he said.

Tabitha rose to her feet as the dragon rolled back over onto his feet and scanned the dim interior of the cave through sleepy eyes with one scaley brow raised slightly as if in question.

"Hello, Zarg," she said, as if she were an invited guest.

Zarg whipped his head around to see who had spoken. He didn't get many visitors. He stared down his long bumpy snout at her and she saw the recognition in his eyes. "You!" he roared, a puff of smoke issuing from his nostrils. "What are you doing here, Witch? Did you come back for more scales? I venture it won't be so easy this time."

Tabitha's blood turned to ice. It was obvious he hadn't forgotten her. She swallowed the lump that had formed in her throat in a big gulp and took a step forward. "I didn't come for your scales, although when you polish them up, they do make wonderful magic mirrors."

A snort of flames shot from Zarg's nostrils in her direction, making her take a step back on instinct, even though her cowl was fireproof.

"Are you after my treasure, then?" the dragon roared.

Stepping forward to regain her ground, Tabitha snapped to attention, even though her legs felt like jelly beneath her. "No, Zarg,"she said, shaking her head. "I've come to ask for your help with something."

Another snort of fire erupted; this one came close enough that she could feel the heat from it in spite of her grandmother's magic in the cowl. "Why would I help you, you thieving witch?" Zarg bellowed.

"I wouldn't expect your assistance without a cost, you silly old fool," Tabitha said, in an attempt to lighten the mood. "I've brought you this delicious rabbit stew as payment for your services. And it's such a small thing that I ask."

Zarg took another sniff of the air, which by this time, was roiling with the delectable smell of her stew. He raised a scaley brow, shooting her a questioning look. "Really?" he said with skepticism. "What is it which you desire from me?"

"Nothing special, or difficult..." she said, reaching into her cowl to pull out the second cauldron, the one in which she'd mixed the ingredients for her spell. (Yes, I know. It might surprise one how much can fit beneath a witch's cowl.) "Just use your dragon's breath to heat this up for me, so it will turn out just right. That's not so hard, is it?"

The dragon eyed her suspiciously. "Are you sure this isn't just another one of your distractions?" he said, issuing forth another snort of flames, which licked at the edges of her cowl. "If you come near my gold, I'll serve you up well-done."

Tabitha held out her open palms and gave him the most innocent look she could muster. "No tricks, I promise," she said. "There's no reason we can't be friends."

"Dragons don't have friends," Zarg said. "Who are you kidding? What did you really come here for?"

"No, really," she said, feeling nervous. That last lick of flame had come a bit too close for comfort. Her grandmother's magic was old and there was no telling how long before it would begin to lose its power. She really didn't want a good burst of dragon's breath to put it to the test. "I just this spell to help me share my stories and make room in my little house, so I can write more. That's all. Please, won't you help me?"

"Bring that stew over here, and I'll think about it," Zarg said.

Tabitha gulped down another large knot which had formed in her throat. "You want me to bring it over there by you?" she said, trying not to let fear be heard in her voice, even though she was trembling inside. "You're next to your treasure, which you warned me to stay away from. How do I know you won't fricassee my fanny and then just eat all the stew?"

"You don't trust me?" the dragon said, raising both scaly brows. "Don't friends have to trust one another?"

"Well," Tabitha said hesitantly, "I suppose they do." She pulled the hood of her cowl as far over her head as she could and approached the cauldron with the stew in it. She'd made enough stew for a dragon and the cauldron was too big for her to lift by the handle, so she bent down and lifted the cauldron up onto her shoulders. "All right. I'll bring it to you."

When she set it down in front of the scaly creature, a poof of smoke issued from his nostrils. "Taste it," he roared. "I want to be sure you didn't poison it."

Tabitha resisted the urge to cower down under the reverberation of his voice, which made the cavern walls rumbled. "I thought friends needed to trust each other," she said, placing her hands on her hips, attempting to display bravery, in spite of her quaking knees.

"I'm still not sure that you ARE my friend. You've gone to an awful lot of trouble just to get me to cook a spell for you." Zarg said, grumbling. "Go on. Taste it!"

Anger flared momentarily inside of Tabitha at the idea that Zarg didn't trust her, but then she thought about sneaking into the lair as a thief on her last visit, deciding that she really couldn't blame him. So, she shrugged her shoulders and took up a ladle-full of rabbit stew, placing it to her lips and tasting it. The rich flavor of rabbit rolled over her tastebuds as she looked up at the dragon. "You know, it's actually pretty good," she said through a mouthful of stew. She held the ladle out to him. "You should have some yourself."

The aroma of the stew wafted from the ladle as Zarg sniffed the air. "Well...," he said hesitantly, "it does smell awfully good." He bent his long scaley neck down low and flicked out a forked lizard tongue out so fast that what she'd left in the ladle was gone before she even realized it. "Oooooh! That is good."

"Then you'll cook my spell in exchange for the stew?" Tabitha asked hopefully.

Zarg didn't reply, but instead scratched his head with a curved black talon.

"What's the matter?" Tabitha asked. "You said you liked the stew, didn't you?"

"I do," said Zarg. "I like it a lot. That's the problem."

Tabitha didn't know what to think now. What Zarg said didn't make sense. "So why is that a problem?" she asked.

"Don't you see?" said Zarg. "I can eat that whole cauldron of stew in no time. What happens when I want more...? And it's good stew. I will want more."

"So, my rabbit stew is too good?" Tabitha said in disbelief. "You won't trade because I didn't cook up enough of it?"

"You couldn't cook up enough. That rabbit stew is so good that if I eat any, I'll be hooked for life... And dragons have very long lives."

Tabitha's heart sank down into a pit deep within her bowels. *How would she ever convince Zarg to cook her spell for her?* Apparently, she had been too successful with her last attempt, and in doing so, had defeated herself.

She gave out a deep sigh. "Isn't there anything I can do to make you change your mind?" she asked without really expecting a positive reply. A tear slid from the corner of her eye and rolled down her cheek. "I made you a whole cauldron full of stew.... What do you want?"

"What do I want?" Zarg said, letting out a huge puff of smoke from his nostrils and tilting his head over to the side. "I don't think I've ever been asked that before. What do I want?"

What had seemed a vast space upon entering, soon felt quite cramped as Zarg began pacing to and fro in the cavern, scratching his head with a curved black talon. She had to hop up in the air each time his tail swished by her.

Suddenly he stopped, turning to stare at her, and Tabitha cowered, feeling prickles of fear up and down her spine.

"You really made a whole cauldron of rabbit stew just for me?" he asked, raising one scaley eyebrow.

Tabitha nodded her head, unsure whether this was a fact that would please or displease the big lizard. She took a step back as he reached out a taloned claw toward her, but the curved portion brushed her cheek, wiping away the tear, which had settled near her nose.

"Why are you crying?" he asked. "Why is the spell so important to you?"

"It was supposed to help me share my stories so people could read them, and I'd have room to create more," Tabitha said, nodding once more.

"Wait," said Zarg with a snort of smoke. "That's all you want? To be able to write and share stories?"

"Yes, that's all I wanted," Tabitha said, nodding again, although now she was beginning to feel a little foolish. "Is that so much to ask?"

"And you made me a delicious rabbit stew," Zarg said, still scratching his scaley head with that one curved black talon, "and risked my wrath, just so you could write and share stories?"

Tabitha sighed, hanging her head. "Yeah, I guess it was a stupid reason," she said, turning to walk away, back the way she had come. She couldn't believe she had gone to all of this trouble for nothing, but she no longer held out hope of changing Zarg's mind.

"Wait!" Zarg bellowed, his voice echoing off the cavern walls and stopping Tabitha in her tracks. "Where do you think you're going?"

Tabitha thought it was obvious, but she replied anyway. "I know when I've lost," she said. "There's no more point in bothering you anymore. I've failed to concoct my spell successfully."

She gathered up the cauldron with the spell and placed it inside her cowl, but she left the cauldron with the stew where it sat. She didn't want to lug the heavy thing back through the forest, so she decided to leave it there for Zarg. At least her stew wouldn't go to waste.

"Stop!" roared the dragon.

Tabitha froze in her tracks. She turned and looked back over her shoulder at Zarg, waiting to feel the heat of his dragon's breath against the back of her cowl. But it didn't come.

"Why don't you share one of your stories with me?" the dragon said in a quieter voice. "I like a good story as much as the next dragon. If it's as good as your rabbit stew, I know I would enjoy it."

She turned around to stare at the big, scaley lizard, who looked rather sad. "You want me to tell you a story?"

Zarg nodded his head. "It gets lonely in this cave. No one ever comes to visit, and when they see me, most people are too scared to even say 'Hello,'" he said, a tear slipping out of his eye and down one scaley cheek. "A good story is just what I need, and you said you wanted to share them."

Tabitha scratched her chin and thought. *The dragon seemed sincere in wanting to hear a story, and she did have a great desire to share them. Telling him a story would seem to meet both of their needs, and besides, a smart witch doesn't refuse the request of a dragon if she knows what's good for her.*

"All right," she said. "Let me bring the stew over by this rock where I can settle in, and you can eat it while I tell you one of my favorites."

Zarg smiled a toothy smile. If you have ever seen a dragon smile, you'll know it's not a pretty sight. The smile that Zarg gave to Tiny Tabby was a downright, out-and-out grin. He moved over to sit next to her to eat his stew and hear her story.

Tabitha told him one of her favorite stories about a princess who was locked in a castle, kept prisoner by a witch's curse, and when she'd finished, the silly dragon was grinning like a lovesick fool.

"I just love happy endings," Zarg said. "That was a good story. Are they all like that?"

"Well, no," Tabitha said. "My stories are each very different, but they are all entertaining. Would you like me to tell you another?"

"I want to hear them all!" said the dragon, with an enthusiasm Tabitha had never heard from him before.

Tabitha scratched her head and thought. Zarg had given her an idea. "If you come home with me, you could hear each one before I send them out into the world," she suggested. "I could create a cave for you out of my back room, once I get all the stories out of there, and you could stay over whenever you want."

She hadn't thought it possible, but Zarg's smile got even bigger than it already was, as he nodded his head enthusiastically. She could see through the spaces between his sharp, pointy, dragon teeth. Puffs of smoke came out of his nostrils and floated up to the cavern ceiling. Apparently, Zarg liked her idea.

So, that is what they did. Tabitha shared her stories, first with Zarg and then with the rest of the world. Her house stayed clean, and she didn't even need to cook her spell. Zarg came and stayed in his cave in the back room whenever he wanted and was never a lonely dragon again.

Kaye Lynne Booth

KAYE LYNNE BOOTH LIVES, works and plays in the mountains of Colorado. As a multi-genre author and founder of *WordCrafter Press*. She has compiled and edited anthologies and collections of short fiction and poetry, as well as editing novels, self-help and spiritual books. Kaye holds an M.F.A. in Creative Writing and is currently seeking an M.A. in Publishing. She was a judge for the 2020 Western Writers of America book awards and served on the editorial team for Western Colorado University and *WordFire Press* for the *Gilded Glass* anthology.

Blog – Writing to be Read: writingtoberead.com

Website – WordCrafter: https://kayebooth.wixsite.com/wordcrafter

COUNTER MELODY

by Meia Holland

EVERYONE KNOWS THE story of Orpheus, the man whose music could move even the gods, and his love for the beautiful Eurydice. Generation after generation have told of how, when Eurydice died on the day of their wedding, Orpheus followed her into the Underworld to win her back. There, moved by Orpheus's music, Hades offered him a deal: Eurydice would follow Orpheus out of the Underworld so long as Orpheus never looked back to check that she was there. If only it had been as easy as it sounded. Orpheus walked up out of the Underworld, but when he couldn't hear Eurydice behind him, the silence made him doubt. Steps away from the realm of the living, his doubt overcame him and he turned to see if she was there. She was. But now Orpheus had broken his deal with Hades, and so the God of the Dead reclaimed her, leaving poor Orpheus alone and bereft.

Yes, everyone knows Orpheus' story.

But what about Eurydice's?

"OK, I KNOW ORPHEUS is deluded when it comes to you," Harpina said as she finally found the clearing Eurydice was sitting in. "But now he seems to have completely lost touch with reality. I mean, when I ran into him just now, he said you'd agreed to *marry* him. Of all things—"

Eurydice turned to face her and the tears running down her friend's face shocked Harpina to silence.

"I did," Eurydice signed, hands shaking.

"But you didn't want to—I know you didn't want to!—so, by all the gods, *why?*"

Eurydice signed frantically as the tears and terror got worse. "He's been after me for so long, convincing everyone that I was just playing hard to get. I thought all he cared about was 'winning'. I thought if I finally gave in and showed some interest, he'd move on! I thought agreeing to marry him would make him lose interest and focus on someone else and I could finally get on with my life, but he's gone to get a priest and witnesses and—"

Her hands balled up into fists, so there went the signing. And now she was sobbing so hard that even if she'd been speaking, there was no way Harpina would have been able to lip read properly. Harpina sank to her knees next to Eurydice and pulled her into a hug. Eurydice might be too far gone to communicate in any way Harpina could understand, but she'd still be able to listen. Harpina rubbed soothing circles on Eurydice's back as she spoke.

"Hey, shh, it's ok—well, ok, it really isn't, but we'll figure something out. He doesn't get to win after everything he's put you through." This wasn't the first time she'd held a crying Eurydice since Orpheus had 'discovered' her, but it was the first time it felt like Eurydice had given up. There was more hopelessness than anger here, and that scared Harpina. "We'll find a way to get you out of this."

Eurydice jerked away, but only far enough to sign, anger in every gesture. Harpina was just glad there was any fight left in her at all.

"There's no way out of this! He's convinced everyone I want him, even my dad, the god of Truth among other things! Not that it'll matter that the truth is that I don't want Orpheus, Dad'll know I'm lying if I said I didn't agree and—"

Wait, that was *it!*

"Eurydice, your dad's Apollo, right?" Harpina interrupted.

"Yeah, but he won't help me. Not only does he think Orpheus is the best thing since the invention of the lyre, the egoist, but if you think he cares at all about the word 'no', why don't you go ask Daphne about what happened to her? Oh wait, you can't. *She turned into a tree to get away from him*. I wish I could turn into a tree..."

"I wasn't thinking of asking your dad for help," Harpina explained. "But, speaking of trees, maybe someone higher up your family tree could help?"

"The Goddesses don't get a say in who my father says I will marry, and as for the Gods? Poseidon won't care enough to go against Apollo on something this 'trivial' and Zeus is even *worse* when it comes to hearing the word 'no'!"

"You're forgetting someone," Harpina said. She knew it would be a tough sell: Demeter was another parent who wouldn't listen. Even when Persephone made her choice, Demeter had made sure that it was Demeter's version of who the villain was that everyone agreed with—never mind who had been the one to actually hold all of humanity hostage.

"Right, 'cause the great uncle who *kidnapped his wife and tricked her into never being able to truly escape him* is going to be *so* helpful here!" All the anger flowed out of Eurydice then, replaced with bitter resignation. "You do make a point, though. There is one escape left. Maybe after I've killed myself, I can drink from the Lethe and forget any of this ever happened."

"No, curse it, that's not your only choice!" Harpina cried. She'd been keeping this card in reserve for years, but if there was ever a time to play it, it was now. "Because that is *not* what happened with Hades and Persephone."

"What do you mean, 'that's not what happened'? *Everyone* knows that's what happened!" Eurydice signed with impatience and incredulity.

"Just like everyone knows you're in love with Orpheus?"

That stopped Eurydice cold. She looked at Harpina for one astonished moment before her expression turned to determination. Much better.

"Tell me," Eurydice signed.

And Harpina did.

"LET ME SEE IF I HAVE this right," Hades said, looking down at the newly dead spirit before him, "after months of being pressured by a man your father, who also happens to be my nephew, approved of—" and why the parents of young women couldn't just actually listen to their daughters, Hades would never know, "—you finally agreed to marry him, thinking he'd leave you alone if you did. After that backfired spectacularly, with the help of a friend, you got a snake to bite you, a snake so poisonous as to be instantly fatal, at which point you came to my realm and presented yourself to me. And that friend was Harpina." Because of course it was. This was *exactly* the kind of thing Harpina would do. "Am I missing anything?"

"No, Lord Hades," Eurydice said, bowing her head in deference. "Though she did also tell me to tell you, 'You owe me and I'm collecting.'"

From her own throne beside Hades, Persephone let out a snort.

Hades raised an eyebrow at her.

"What?" his wife said, raising an eyebrow right back. "She's right: we do owe her. And if this is how she wants to call in that debt, I'm happy to oblige."

Hades sighed. She was right, of course. If it hadn't been for Harpina's willingness to smuggle their letters back and forth and play a key role in the distraction that finally let Persephone escape her mother's, uh, opinions—"No daughter of mine is marrying the God of the Dead and living in his realm!"—he wouldn't be sitting with his wonderful wife today.

They did owe her. And they were going to pay her back.

"Well, love, do you have any room for a new attendant?" He doubted Eurydice would want a place among his, mostly male, attendants, and there was no way he was repaying the debt he owed Harpina by making her friend a general palace servant.

"There's always room for one more," Persephone said, giving Eurydice a welcoming smile.

"Very well," Hades said, turning back to face Eurydice. "Be welcome in my palace and among my lady's attendants."

"Come on," Persephone said, getting up and bending over to give him a quick kiss on the cheek before descending from the dais and taking Eurydice's arm. "Let's go walk in the gardens and talk."

Hades watched them leave and reflected on the palace gardens. They'd grown so much since Persephone had become his wife. That hadn't been surprising—he'd known he was marrying the Goddess of Spring after all. No, what had been surprising was what she's made the garden out of. It had its share of regular plants, of course, with the pomegranate trees—*their* pomegranate trees—in pride of place, but most of the garden was filled with plants she'd made of the things of his realm. Vines of gold, growing flowers with ruby petals.

She'd called it a way to spit in the eye of anyone who said they didn't belong together. He'd called it beautiful. Even now, they worked on it together when they could. Those precious hours in the gardens were one of the highlights of her visits, the half of the year they were allowed to be happy together.

He was deep in these musings when a guard entered the throne room with a report of what had just happened at the River Styx.

Cold settled through him at the news, and he sent for Persephone and Eurydice. It wasn't the cold of fear or the emptiness of despair. No, this cold *burned*. It was fury.

"What happened?" Persephone asked, panting as she leaned on the doorway. They must have sprinted to get here. Eurydice didn't need to breathe anymore, of course, but the fear in her eyes told him she knew why she'd been called. That fear made the fury burn colder.

"Someone stole Charon's boat and crossed the River Styx after singing him to sleep." Persephone's eyes lit with understanding as Eurydice sunk in on herself. "Orpheus has broken into my realm, and he hasn't paid the toll. There will be *consequences.*"

"He's come to take me back, hasn't he?" Eurydice whispered, and it wasn't a question. "Even in death, I can't escape him."

"*No,*" Hades hissed. "You are dead, and *my* subject. He has no claim on you now—not that he ever did. I will *not* hand you over to him."

"More than that!" Persephone snapped, her rage running hot. "You are *my* attendant. I will not stand for you being handed over like some lost possession!"

"You say that now..." Eurydice said, her eyes going very far away and her shoulders slumping in defeat. For all their promises, she was giving up. Why?

"You doubt us?" Hades asked, doing his best to keep his voice level.

"No, Lord Hades, my apologies," Eurydice said, bowing her head again and lying through her teeth. Clearly, she didn't think they would follow through.

"If you do believe us, then why do you act as if you don't?"

Eurydice looked away, but Hades said nothing. He let the silence grow, pulling the truth out of her.

"I've seen this too many times before," Eurydice finally said, still not looking at either of the Gods. "He will sing, and you will believe his story. It's what happened every time. Gods, mortals, it doesn't matter. He'll convince you and take me back and I'll spend the rest of eternity listening to him talk about how he won me back from the dead. My words have never meant anything compared to his songs. The only person I've ever known to not be taken in by him is Harpina, and she's deaf."

"And you," Hades pointed out.

"No," Eurydice replied, shaking her head. "Even I liked his music once. Before it was about me."

Persephone looked at him, eyes blazing. "Candle wax."

Hades blinked at her, some of his fury fading in the face of confusion. "Pardon?"

"Candle wax," Persephone repeated. "It worked for Odysseus's crew; it should work for us." She turned back to Eurydice and grabbed her hands. "We'll stuff our ears with it and won't be able to hear a note. If you're so certain that if we hear his music we'll believe him, then we won't take that risk. We'll put candle wax in our ears, and he'll never come near you again."

"He's a living man in the land of the dead," Hades added. "There are things that could be done to him." Sisyphus and Tantalus were example enough that he could create a punishment that fit the crime. "We could arrange some revenge, if that's what you desire."

"We're not letting you go, Eurydice. Not with him," Persephone reassured her. "Tell us what you want us to do to him."

"Actually," Eurydice said, looking between the two of them. "I think there's something I can do that would hurt him the most. Here's what we'd need to do."

Hades and Persephone listened to her plan, and by the end of it, they were smiling. Let the punishment fit the crime indeed.

EURYDICE WALKED A FEW stops behind Orpheus, up the path that everyone eventually went down, and few but Persephone walked up again. In her hand she held the golden vine Persephone had given her, to reel her in once she'd broken Orpheus. Once Orpheus had broken himself. The only two rules he'd been given were that he could not turn and look at her and he could not speak. If he couldn't talk over her or ignore her words while undressing her with his eyes, his only choice would be to listen, and that was the one thing he could never do.

"I used to love your music, you know," she started. The higher he was, the harder he'd fall, and the truth of it made the whole thing that much worse. "I used to go to all your concerts. My dad is Apollo, after all; I know good music when I hear it. I used to look forward to them, once upon a time." Orpheus started to turn his head to look back at her over his shoulder, but stopped himself. He cocked it instead. Good, he was finally *listening.* "Of course, that all stopped when you noticed me and turned my life into a living nightmare."

He nearly tripped, and she snorted. It wasn't a happy sound.

"I told you," she said, as he kept walking. "Over and over, and *over* again, I told you I wasn't interested, that I didn't want you, that what I *did* want was to be left alone, but you *never listened.* Now? Now you have no choice." He'd never given her one, after all. "Every time I pushed you away, you'd come back harder. You started getting other people to court me for you. By the end, there was nowhere I could go without someone trying to convince me to admit how I really felt about you and stop playing so hard to get, no one I could ask for help who wouldn't tell you where I was hiding. You got to all of them." All of them except Harpina, whom he'd never even really noticed. Why would he, when she couldn't care less about music she couldn't hear and judged him on his actions instead? But Eurydice kept her only mortal ally's name hidden in her heart. Orpheus had already proved what he could do to sway the crowd. Setting all the anger he could bring to bear against Harpina would be a poor repayment for everything she had done. "You even turned my father against me when I called on him for help."

Orpheus had sung Apollo a song, and he'd loved it. It had been one of Orpheus' least veiled works, one that left Eurydice feeling dirty every time she'd heard it. Apollo had laughed. Laughed, and congratulated Orpheus on his clever use of words and music and made it clear to both of them that Orpheus had his blessing in his hunt. It didn't matter what

Eurydice had said and kept saying. He wouldn't *listen*. None of them would.

The helplessness of that memory turned to blinding rage bubbling behind her breastbone. This had gone on for far too long already. It was time, and past time to go for the throat.

"I hate you now, you know," she told him. "I've hated you for a long time. I only ever agreed to marry you because I thought that once you had what you wanted—or as close to what you wanted as I was willing to give, I mean, since the thought of you actually touching me made me sick, I didn't have many other options but agree to one of your proposals—you would move on to some other poor girl who just wanted a fun night listening to pretty music with her friends, and I could get on with my life. And when that backfired spectacularly," thank you Hades, "I killed myself to escape." Harpina had been the one to find the snake and lure it in, but it was Eurydice who got it to bite her. "The pain from the fangs and the venom felt like freedom. It didn't matter that I would be dead, I would be away from *you*. And then you followed me down here and ruined that, too. I know you never loved me, but is there *nothing* you wouldn't do to hurt me?"

"*Hurt you?!*" Orpheus snapped, turning around. For the first time in months, Eurydice smiled. "Eurydice, I followed you into the *Underworld!* HOW CAN YOU BELIEVE I DON'T LO— "He froze then, his voice echoing in the tunnel, his eyes locked on hers. Two simple rules and he'd broken them both, and they both knew it.

"Because if you really did love me," Eurydice replied, "you would have listened to me the first time I told you no. Because if you loved me, you would have listened to anything I ever had to say. And because if you loved me, you wouldn't have let your pride get the better of you and broken your deal to try to make me shut up again. You don't love me, and you never did. Goodbye, Orpheus. I hope you live a long and miserable life before you return here. Don't try to find me when you do."

And with that, she gave the vine two quick tugs and felt Hades start to pull her spirit back to where it belonged. Back where she was safe, and people listened to the truth and blocked out lies with candle wax.

Orpheus fell to his knees as she was pulled away, and let out a scream of pure rage and despair. Eurydice smiled. For the first time since all this started, his voice was music to her ears.

Meia Holland

MEIA HOLLAND IS A 26-year-old queer Montrealer with a passion for stories about love and relationships in all their forms

Once Upon a Time, and Now, and Forever

by Lyndsay E. Gilbert

I WORK HARD TO BECOME her. Night and day I warp myself, twisting and writhing until my form models her exactly. Narrow hips, slender brown arms, each long, gracefully tapered finger, two strong legs, two small, round breasts, the smattering of freckles across her cheeks-an arcane constellation.

I read her like mages read the skies. I know the alignment of each fleck of green in the dark, wide-set pools of her eyes. I mimic the pout of her dry, cracked lips, imagining I might open them and form the words she speaks, like I might become an echo too, a being made of sound as well as sight.

I practice and practice.

I watch her every moment that I can through my single window to her world. Eventually the Elders realise I belong to her, and she belongs to me. I am granted the position of being her sole reflection in the full-length, ornate mirror in her bedroom. It is her most important reflection, for it is here in that she gazes most often in the mirror. Each morning maids fuss around and dress her for the day, but more intimately at night, alone, she stares and stares, explores, examines, enjoys the secrets of her body.

I am with her then. My Faceless sisters join me in the mornings, reflecting the bustling maids. With the busy ritual done and the chamber empty, we all fade back into the Nowhere.

But I alone return to her come eventide. My sisters are sorely jealous. I am hated and ignored by them, but I care little. I am the princess' reflection now and forced to be no one else.

My skill grows. The Elders give me the power to slip between mirrors, to appear in the waters, and the darkened panes of window glass, going wherever the princess goes, whether she peers into a shining surface, or simply passes it by.

I am always there.

FLOATING IN THE NOWHERE, I perfect the length of the princess' nails. She has taken to wearing them long and pointed. I hold up one hand to appreciate my work, but I overhear a voice.

Let her enjoy the last of it. Soon her pretty princess will be dead.

We Faceless have no true voices; all our words are merely thoughts we deign to share. I swim through our astral home toward the source of the words ringing in my mind. My sisters are gossiping, so formless that they merge momentarily in the places where they touch. Seven void-black clouds huddled together.

"Who says the princess will die?" I demand.

Their chatter dries up, replaced by soft laughter.

"I will ask the Elders then. They should know how you speak of our sacred duties." I turn as if to go there right away and expose their frivolity. My threat works.

You are young and naïve yet. Her stepmother plans to poison her. Don't you know this story?

The form of the princess sloughs off me, returning me to my truth, just another cloud-like mass. But tendrils trail away from me like grey smoke from a doused flame. I cannot accept this fate, cannot allow my princess to be poisoned.

My maid will be the one to administer it. My eldest sister quivers with the joy of it. More laughter, gleeful, cruel. I soar away from them. Soon it will be late.

Carefully I drift into the mirror's silver expanse, making myself like air, invisible. I'm just a little early. I only need a moment of peace. Time to think about what I can do to help my princess. Time to contemplate everything I *want* to do.

All of it forbidden.

THE ROOM ITSELF REQUIRES no Faceless beings to reflect it in the mirror. Only living things, creatures with souls, need us. We take their form and cradle their essence, holding it deep inside where it is safe from the abyss of the Nowhere.

I do not know where we come from, what we really are. But I hold on to the fact that we are important, hold it with as much tender care as I do the soul of the princess.

She enters the room in a hurry, slamming the door. The core of her sinks into the core of me. Now I may move as she does, in perfect time and perfect motion.

I am no longer mere smoke; I am almost matter. I feel the heat of a fire in the grate, tickling her skin. The flames leap in her irises, a reflection in a reflection. Even though she does not look directly into the mirror, I still mimic every detail, every experience.

Unease grips her. A tightness in her chest as she takes small, erratic breaths. A dragging sensation, like some ghostly hand is trying to pull her heart into her stomach. She massages her temples and takes several deep breaths. The turmoil settles. Finally, she comes to me.

"I can do this," she says. I love the husky resonance of her voice. I covet the sound waves she makes, want to capture them and hold them inside me, the way I hold her soul. Her soul has a color, more vibrant than any I have known-a deep, pulsing red. I imagine it is a heart, that I am human, and it is pumping crimson blood through my veins, bringing me to life.

"He will return soon, and I will tell him everything." She stands taller, holds her head higher. "Father, I'll say. There will be no prince. I have found my soulmate." She nods decisively. "Just like that. I can do this." Her voice trembles and she clears her throat. "Be strong like Mother."

She needs to know the truth. I must tell her about the poison, the treacherous maid. I disobey the rules. Her soul burns hot as I reach my hand up to touch the glass. She staggers back, grabbing a wooden bedpost for support. Her soul twists and contorts, hotter and hotter it grows, scalding me inside as it tries to regain control. I channel every ounce of my willpower to confine it, to withstand the pain and the high-pitched song of its terror as it realizes I am winning.

I press my other hand to the glass and project my words into her mind. *I came to warn you. Your stepmother plans to murder you, to-*

The door opens and a maid enters. My eldest sister manifests at my side. I stop my rebellion, falling back under the influence of the princess's soul, now roiling like clouds in a stormy sky. The princess steps closer to the mirror, eyes narrowed. She bites into her bottom lip, and the taste of copper floods her tongue. I obey every movement. She draws her fingers down the glass, as if trying to caress me.

"Your highness?" The maid moves toward the princess and my sister floats closer to me. "Are you alright?"

The princess's soul is slippery and eel-like, eager to get away from me. I pray to whatever Faceless gods exist, pray the princess does not tell her maid what she has seen.

Regardless, it is done now. I must commit to my plans and play this out. I control my words with utmost precision, ensuring they only go into the princess's mind. *Say nothing of me and I will protect you.*

She frowns, her hand drops to her side, and she steps back from the mirror. "Just a taxing day," she tells the maid.

"I will bring you a soothing tea."

A telltale tremor weakens her voice. At my side, my sister leaks excitement into the space around us. It fills up the entire frame until I swear, I must be swimming in it as I match the princess's tight smile.

"I would like that very much," she says.

The maid bobs an unsteady curtsey and leaves the room. My sister dissipates back into the Nowhere. She hasn't earned the allowances or cultivated my power. She cannot stay in the mirror unless she has a soul to hold. Nor can she go from mirror to mirror, surface-to-surface. She serves only this mirror.

I am alone with the princess again, and I *will* save her. *Your maid will bring poisoned tea. You must not drink it.*

She tilts her head, a delicate, birdlike gesture as she hears my words again. She comes close to the mirror once more. I force my arms to disobey and hold them out as if I might embrace her.

"Mayhap I'm already poisoned, and this is some fever dream." Her face is paler, sickly, but she is brave. "Who are you?" she asks.

I'm not a who, I am a what. Still, hearing those words sends a cold thrill of familiarity through me.

I am Sorcha. Where does this name come from? I surely invented it just now. We Faceless have no names. We strive not to matter, perfect being anything and everything but our own selves.

"Have you come from the future?" Her gaze is hungry now. "Are you a fae? A djinn? Something here to change my world."

I want so desperately to be the thing that satisfies the hunger in her eyes. *I came to save your life. That's all you need to know right now.*

She raises her thick, arched eyebrows. "Why should I trust you? And when I refuse this poison, what will my stepmother do next?"

Her maid will return soon, my sister with her. She will know that I interfered, and she will tell the Elders. Everything I worked for will crumble away. A wicked longing rises from the depths of me.

Something I've been carrying inside, afraid to acknowledge. Her soul shrinks away, sensing the arrival of this force.

Sorcha.

I want to have a name.

I want to have a body.

Her body.

Break the mirror. Break it and I will come through. Break it and I will rescue you.

She glances at the door. "My mother told me that breaking a mirror shatters your soul."

I sense my sister's presence coming nearer. *That is mere superstition*, I lie, even as I cradle her soul. *For seven years, I can keep you safe. That is the true power of it. Break it now or face your doom. I can help you escape the fate your stepmother has planned for you.*

She holds her breath. My sister starts to materialize as the door handle turns. It's over.

Crack.

The princess smashes her fist into the glass. My sister flickers away, unable to withstand the violent rupture.

In the centre of my being, the princess' soul splinters into pieces. A hundred silver knives carve it apart at once. The pulsing, vibrant red of it fades to raw pink. I release my hold on it as I drop the princess' form. The jagged cracks in the mirror scrape against me as I slip through them and pour out into the real world. I make straight for the princess's body, now an empty sack to be filled.

Around me, her soul floats through the air, pieces of chaos, a school of captured fish swimming aimlessly in the cage of a net. They dart at her body, my body, trying to get back in. I repel them with strength and desire and conviction.

I said I would keep her safe and I will. In my own way.

The maid enters the room. I am on the floor at the base of the broken mirror, skirts pooled around me. My hand is cut and bleeding.

"Your highness!" the maid cries.

She does not drop her wicked cup of poison, does not run to me. Each broken fragment in the mirror frame holds one of my sisters. All of them are needed now. They reflect the maid over and over.

I imagine their confusion, but they must obey the soul they are sharing. Perhaps the way they have been merging in the Nowhere has prepared them for this moment.

Now, let them see what *I* can do.

I get to my feet, ignoring every attempt of the Princess's soul to enter and dethrone me. Soon it will grow tired. Soon it will understand it needs every drip of energy for the battle coming next.

Seven years. The exact amount of time it takes for a soul to regenerate.

The maid approaches with the tea held out before her, hands shaking. Her eyes widen as I pass her by and slam the bolt across the door, closing us in together.

"I feel a lot better." It is glorious to hear my words in the air, born from the power of my lungs and the instrument of my throat. A real voice. "But you are unsettled now, my dear. You should drink the tea instead."

Before she can pretend to spill it, I come close to her, close enough to see little beads of sweat on her forehead. I grip the cup in one hand and force it to her lips, grasping her by the elaborate knots in her hair. She scrapes me with her fingernails and seals her lips together. I drag her to the bed and push her down. Tea sloshes hot over my hand and I grip the cup tighter as I straddle her, pinching her nose closed.

She convulses beneath me like a body possessed and I squeeze my thighs, riding out every jolt and spasm until finally she opens her mouth, gasping. I pour the tea in, then jam her mouth shut, one hand covering her lips, the other holding her jaw.

She chokes and gulps. Tears leak from the edges of her bloodshot blue eyes. I slide off her and she coughs. Bright red blood trickles from her mouth and runs down the side of her face. She mewls, pathetic and weak, before going still, eyes staring upward.

I look back at the broken mirror, knowing my Faceless sisters will be gone now. A corpse is like any soulless object. But when I see her questing soul, I remember what I am. Her soul floats above her body, a pale blue hue, then it streams toward the window. But the window is closed, and the mirror shards already have the soul in their hold.

A doorway opens inside me, long closed, tightly locked away. But I walk through it now, and I remember.

I remember, and it hurts.

"SORCHA!" MY LITTLE sister's scream. I am slipping away under my drunken brother's bloodied fists.

My mother crawls across the hard dirt floor of our cottage. "What have you done, Darragh? What have you done?"

"I'm sorry." My last words, voice a frail thing, soft and high. I rise out of my small, hungry, peasant body, not sad to go. Secretly desperate. Terribly guilty.

The pride and joy of the family, a rugged little mirror from my mother's dowry, hangs above the fireplace, something my father and brother have not yet sold away for whiskey. It calls to me, a gentle questioning hum at first. The promise of belonging. I look at the single dirty window, high up, near the thatched roof. I need to get to the sky. I need to fly up to heaven, but I can't.

"Open the door! Cover that damnable mirror!" My mother's cries are frantic but come too late. The mirror's call is overpowering and even as it draws me in, I start to forget.

I never had a name. Never had a voice. Never had a face.

Except I did.

NOW I RUN TO THE BEDROOM window and try to shove it open. Not even a poisoner deserves to become what I have become. The frame is stiff. By the time the cold night air flutters through the curtains, the maid's soul is gone, no longer even in the mirror. It is somewhere in the Nowhere, forgetting who it is, learning its new purpose.

The princess's soul remains with me, tremulously attached to this body. Not dead and not alive. The shreds of her still pummel into me. I can no longer see them, except in the mirror shards. I realise with a start that I no longer have a reflection.

A strong breeze rushes through the room, drying the sweat on my skin. I look out the window, up at the blue-black sky and the swollen white moon. I could leave this body. I could rise toward heaven. I could be free.

But I am too afraid. Too desperate for life.

I wrap my stolen arms around my stolen body and turn away from the window.

THE QUEEN DENIES HER part in the poisoning attempt, but she does not dare question the death of the maid.

"Imagine serving always, never being at the centre of anything," she says, waving one hand airily, the other playing with her toffee-coloured curls. "She must have broken inside."

I force myself to meet her cinnamon brown eyes. How close she is to the truth.

I insisted my shattered mirror be removed and not replaced. I tread through the palace with great care, avoiding all reflective surfaces. If my lack of reflection is discovered, they may burn me alive as a changeling or witch.

I promised the princess I would keep her safe.

A rasping whisper makes me glance behind. There are no mirrors or fountains in the throne room. I cannot check what the princess' soul is doing. She can't have figured out the mind words, not yet.

The queen reaches over and takes the king's hand. They sit side by side on twin thrones. Stepmother. Step-queen. Whatever she is, she has the king's ear.

"Daughter," he beckons, and I go to him. He stands and draws me into a strong, warm embrace that smells of melted sugar and figs. Tears prick my eyes and I blink them away along with the flashes of my own father's violence. I never felt this once, the safe circle that a father's arms should be.

Mi-mi-miiine.

I stiffen, pulling away. He kisses my forehead all the same and then sits again. "Aoife thinks it is long past time we considered all the suitors vying for your hand."

I fight not to look behind me for the voice again. I cannot allow her to disturb me like this. I manage to nod. Mayhap getting out of this palace is the right thing. The alternative is waiting while the queen makes further plans for my demise.

M-m-my de-mi... She does not manage the full word, but goosebumps erupt along my skin. I feel breath on the back of my neck, close and hot and humid.

This is mere fancy, impossible, a trick of my fear.

"My young cousin, Finn, is most interested," the queen says. "I will invite him to stay with us in the coming month."

Most interested in my murder, no doubt. I smile demurely and curtsey. My father dismisses me, winking as I turn to leave his presence. The princess does not speak again, but I swear I can read her thoughts.

He is not your father. He is my father.

Everything belongs to me.

I DISMISS MY MAIDS and head out alone to the gardens, straight past the rows of flowers, blooming autumn colors, fast along the well-kept pathways that run through the perfect stretches of lawn. I reach my destination out of breath. An ancient fountain on the border between the vast forest and the palace grounds.

A marble statue of a forgotten harvest goddess creates the centerpiece. She cradles a skull in one arm and a bushel of wheat in the other. All around her hands reach up from the underworld, supplicants grasping her skirts.

The water is unmoving, for the fountain broke long ago. I step closer and stare down into its stillness. I am not reflected, but just behind the place where I should be is the soul of the princess. A horrific, broken thing. It has tried to take on her likeness, but the fleshy pink color keeps seeping through like watery blood. It looks like a patchwork doll made of human pieces, stitched together by a child. Each part does not match up. The face keeps sliding off.

"There you are!"

I scream as a young woman steps out of the woods. She rushes to my side and before I can speak. She takes my face in her strong, rough hands and presses her lips to mine. The shock subsides when I close my eyes. My first kiss. She tastes of winterberries; her tongue is soft and cool against mine.

When she draws back, I long for more, but I do not even know her name. There are pieces of the princess's life that are a secret, even from her own reflection.

I have found my soulmate. I recall how she talked to herself. This is what she wanted to tell her father.

The woman's eyes rove over my face. She is tall and hale with a muscular body like that of a boy. She dresses like a boy too, except for her beautiful blonde hair, cascading unbound around her. A silver hunting horn hangs at her hip. She works for the palace.

So much for the queen's cousin, for all those nameless suitors. Which of them could ever compete with this striking huntress?

"I thought about everything you said, Cloda. I waited every day for you to come. I heard about the poison."

Cloda. The princess has a name. Of course she has a name. "I saved myself." I almost blunder the words, my tongue heavy with the lie.

"Yes, you did." She smiles, a wry twist of her berry-stained lips. "And it's time to save yourself again. Come with me. Save yourself now and every day after."

I glance at the water. The princess is reaching out towards the huntress; her face featureless, a melting brown expanse, but her twisted hands hold enough emotion for me to read. Longing. Desperation.

Thief.

Her voice is clear and thunders through me. I look to the huntress. She is staring into the water, her mouth agape. "What..." Her voice trails away, and she turns to me. "What are you?"

Her hand goes to her hip, and I notice a wicked-looking dagger sheathed beside the horn, half hidden by her long coat. She pulls it out and I back away.

I must fight her.

I must kill her.

But she doesn't come at me. Instead, she clutches her own head, and glances about in fear. Dread blossoms from my centre and trickles out into every part of me, all that is mine and all that is stolen.

The princess is speaking to her.

"Please," I say. "You must understand. I came to help her. She's broken now."

You tricked me. You took my body for yourself. But what happens if she cuts you out of me? Her words are shuddering rage.

The huntress stalks toward me and I back away, toward the edge of the woods. "If you kill this body, no one can use it," I warn. "Wait seven years and she will be ready again to enter it."

I am ready now! she screams. *And if not, I'd rather be dead than be like this. I will take my chances. Will you take yours?*

I turn and run into the forest, the shattered princess at my heels like a hellhound, waiting to be whole, waiting to destroy me.

But seven years is enough.

Seven years is a lifetime.

I will hold on.

Soon the piercing note of a hunting horn echoes through the trees.

You cannot run from us.

But I do. I run and I run. My faceless sister's words return to me, echoing through my mind, carried on a chorus of malevolent laughter.

Don't you know this story?

ONCE UPON A TIME, DEEP in the dark woods, there lived a witch with no reflection. A witch with a stolen body, a hunger that could not be sated and a wretched, monstrous creature at her back. It stalked her daily like a shadow, always getting closer.

Every seven years, the witch lured a pretty girl into her ramshackle cottage.

She cut herself apart and shed her stolen skin. Climbed like a spider into a fresh and lovely body.

She buried the old one under a stunted yew tree, always with a small broken mirror clutched in its death-pale hands.

The shadow creature transformed with each new body, but always it returned, always it dogged her steps, inching closer.

And the witch lived once upon a time, and now, and forever.

Lyndsay E. Gilbert

LYNDSAY E. GILBERT hails from Northern Ireland, where she lives beside an ancient castle looking out to sea. She loves reading, writing, horror, fantasy, fairy tales, playing the fiddle, cats, dogs (particularly German Shepherds), moving music, cross-stitch, and belly dancing. She has a few stories published in anthologies.

Flipped

By Olivia Merchiston

"ANOTHER DAY IN PARADISE," Hazel grumbled as the small panes of warped glass rattled loudly in their black lead frames. Her cottage, despite standing for hundreds of years in the wilds of Scotland, was *not* a fan of storms. And this was a storm and a half. For days now the wind had howled, the rain pelted against the walls, and the trees around the house struggled to stay upright. Everything outside was messy; debris rushed past as she stared out of the small, deep-set window above her kitchen sink and sighed.

"Yep, another day in paradise. Let's see if we can figure out this spell."

A loud thud and a scratching noise sounded from the lone door. Hazel wrapped her thick-knitted cardigan tighter around herself and went to open it. Along with a strong gust of wind, several leaves and small twigs, and a surprising amount of rain, a large black wolf entered the cottage.

"Willow, for the love of the moon, you're dripping all over the floor!" Hazel cried with an exasperated flounce of her arms. "I have just cleaned in here and then you come in and—"

"All right, all right, I'm sorry. I didn't want to transform outside, though. My fur is so much better against the rain than this stupid human skin," Willow scoffed as their body twisted and warped, cracked and popped, until eventually, a very tall, very muscular figure stood where the wolf once did. Hazel's mouth dried up.

"Very naked," Hazel whispered as her thoughts ran away with her.

"I'm sorry?" Willow raised a quizzical brow and gave her a lopsided smile.

"Hmm?" Hazel managed to slowly drag her eyes up the distracting figure of her familiar until she made eye contact with dark brown eyes that sparkled with mischief. "Nothing. You're just very naked, as usual... Do you mind?"

Willow looked down at themself and, with a wave of their hand, a simple black outfit appeared over their body. She had never seen Willow in anything other than a thin black tee-shirt and simple black trousers. They didn't even wear shoes. Ever.

"Oh!" Willow suddenly exclaimed and began spinning about on the spot like a mad thing. "I brought you... I brought youuuuu... I brou—ah! Here it is. Brought you this; I know you need it."

Hazel watched a blurry object fly towards her and land with a thud on the rough wooden table in front of her. With a small, surprised grin, she shot a look at Willow, who winked back.

"This is what you were doing in this weather? Are you mad? What if you get sick?" Hazel tried to admonish them, but she couldn't help her smile.

"I'm a wolf, Haze. A little rain won't make me sick. And anyway, you used all the last one and you can't make the spell work without it. So, just shut up and say thank you and let's get to work. Ok?"

Hazel's chest flooded with warmth. No matter how many years they'd been with her now, Willow was always surprising her. To think they would go out in this weather just to make sure she could complete her work! She was a lucky witch with a very supportive familiar. She couldn't possibly articulate all of that, though; it was far too embarrassing, so she merely smiled, nodded and said, "Ok. Thank you, Willow."

She picked up the soaking wet, very dead rabbit and moved over to the kitchen counters. She needed to prepare all her ingredients with the utmost focus if this was going to work this time. All the books said this spell was hard, but this would be her *sixteenth* attempt, and she was getting frustrated.

As she pulled dried herbs, candles, and questionable bottles from their respective shelves, she glanced over her shoulder to see Willow settling down in front of the wood-burning stove with a book in their hands. Their long legs stretched out as they sat down, propping their huge bare feet up on the low coffee table and sinking back into the cracked, worn leather of the wingback chair.

"I still don't know why you're bothering with this. You look fine," they said as they glanced up and caught her watching them.

Hazel snapped her eyes back to the pile of ingredients, a blush forming on her cheeks. She hadn't been staring at Willow's large hands and muscled forearms. Nope, not she.

"It's not about how I look now," she sighed. "It's about how I'll look in fifty years when you still look exceptional and I'm... wizened and arthritic and probably incontinent."

Willow laughed, and it filled the small cottage like music.

"I won't feel any different about you then than I do now, Haze. You don't have to do this for my sake."

I'd like it if you felt some kind of different about me, to be honest, Hazel thought as she collected her things and headed over to the side table near the front door. She ran through everything she needed once more in her head: basil, horsetail, distilled water, a rabbit heart (*gross*), sage to burn, candles, a mirror, and lastly, the book containing the incantation she needed to recite as she mixed the ingredients before drinking.

"Ok, it's all ready and I'm going to try really, *really* hard this time, so stay quiet. You distracted me last time," she told Willow with a slightly nervous flap of her hands.

"Pfft, I did no such thing," Willow chuckled as they flipped a page over in their book. "I was coming home from a hunt. How was I to know you wouldn't be able to focus on your work once I transformed?"

"You just had to transform right in my line of sight though, didn't you? What did you think would happen?!"

"You're right," Willow conceded with a serious nod. "Ten years and you still can't keep your eyes in your skull when I transform."

Hazel shot them a harsh glare in the reflection of the large mirror. They weren't wrong, but still, the arrogance. Willow snorted a laugh and returned to their book, allowing Hazel to take a deep, calming breath and centre her mind on the task at hand. Slowed ageing was never something she thought she'd be dealing with, but then she never thought she'd have such an attractive familiar, whose species aged much slower than humans. A lot could go wrong with this spell, as she'd learnt the hard way the first fifteen times. Still, she was adamant that Willow would not be the only super-hot, young-looking eighty-year-old in this house, so she persevered.

She lit the candles, cleansed the area with the sage, and followed the recipe to the letter as she added the various ingredients to a wide-necked glass bottle. As she spoke the incantation, the storm outside seemed to fade away, and she felt her energy shifting and changing as the words echoed around the small cottage. Her eyes flashed with various colours as the magic around her began to work, and once she was done chanting, she lifted the bottle to her lips, took a steadying breath, and drank.

In the mirror, she watched herself intently. The spell slowed the ageing process, but it should also give her a little bit of a 'freshen-up' now. That's how she would know it had worked. The residual magic still swirled in her eyes, mixing dozens of colours in a marbled pattern that she'd always found fascinating.

But nothing else happened.

Her eyes flicked to Willow's reflection, who was still as a statue, book in one hand and the other halfway through turning a page. It didn't even seem as if they were breathing. They watched her so closely that even a rogue strand of their tousled black hair falling into their face didn't distract them from Hazel's reflection.

Still, nothing happened.

It didn't work... again.

Hazel clamped her eyes shut against the disappointment. What had she done so wrong that nothing at all happened? At least the last time she failed, she'd had to live with someone else's nose for a week. But *nothing* happening was an entirely new, and deeper, failure.

She bent to blow out the candles.

"Wow!"

At the sudden exclamation, Hazel nearly jumped out of her skin, while Willow was suddenly on their feet, body twitching and cracking—readying itself to transform—and growling low.

"What the hell?!" Hazel cried as she turned in Willow's direction. But clearly it wasn't them, and as they nodded once towards the mirror behind her, Hazel got a sinking feeling in her gut. She turned slowly on her heel.

"This place is so cute, oh my goodness," a voice said. Hazel's voice. Hazel's reflection's voice. Her reflection was no longer... well, reflecting, and was instead, standing in the mirror with a huge dopey grin on her face. Hazel was speechless. What the hell had she done?!

"Ooh, look at that candle, sweet!" the reflection cooed as she stuck her hand forward, out of the mirror, and reached towards the still alight candle. Her fingers made contact with the flame.

"Ow! Gah, burnie! You should warn folk about that," she said as she flapped her sore hand and then glanced around at the frame of the mirror. Before Hazel could even comprehend what was happening, the reflection's hands were grasping the edges and hauling herself out of the frame. She clattered onto the side table as she tried to find her footing, and her boots, which matched Hazel's exactly, skittered across the polished wooden surface, knocking everything else off.

Hazel watched for what felt like years as her reflection tried to gain her footing. It took an awkwardly long time for her to even get one leg successfully out of the mirror, with her grunting and puffing as she went. Hazel shot a look at Willow, who was still twitching and had their hands clenched tightly into fists, on alert. They glanced back at her and shrugged slightly, but she could see they still weren't relaxing as they watched the reflection flail and puff.

The reflection continued to struggle her way out of the frame. She cursed under her breath now and then, but giggled at her situation, too. Hazel watched for a few more minutes until she couldn't take it anymore.

"Can I... Do you need a hand?" she asked politely.

The reflection, who was now balanced on her hands against the frame, with both feet skittering across the table surface like a newborn deer on ice, paused and looked over her shoulder. She offered Hazel a sheepish grin and said, "That would be great, thanks!"

Hazel stepped forward and offered her a hand. The reflection tried to take it, but as she reached out, her feet slipped again and instead, both she and Hazel went tumbling to the ground, knocking over the side table in the process. Hazel let out an *"oof"* as her body made contact with the stone floor.

"Oh, my lord, I am so sorry!" the reflection cried as she tried to push herself off Hazel. This person, or whatever she was, had no sense of personal space though, as she placed a hand on Hazel's face to push herself up. Hazel just lay there and let her cheek be smashed into the floor in resignation.

"Ok, why don't I help you up, miss?" Willow's voice finally sounded and then suddenly the weight was gone from Hazel's chest and face, and she was able to sit up. Willow had the reflection by the waist, her feet dangling a few inches off the floor.

The reflection bounced around in Willow's hold with that same dopey grin on her face.

"Oooh, strong! I bet I can't get away. Watch this."

With no further warning, she started flailing about uncontrollably in Willow's grip, causing them to throw their head side to side and lean back to avoid her wild arms. Hazel, however, was not so lucky, and in attempting to stand, she caught the reflection's foot right on her chin and fell back to the floor again.

"Haze!"

Willow all but launched the reflection away from them and crouched down to examine Hazel's chin for any damage. Hazel couldn't stop the warm, smug feeling spreading in her chest that they'd so unceremoniously, and quite literally, dumped the reflection at the first sign of her discomfort. And she definitely couldn't stop herself from watching their dark eyes as they looked over her face with worry.

"Does it hurt anywhere?" Willow asked quietly as their hands ran over her jaw softly. The sheer size and power Willow had, Hazel found herself stunned by their ability to be so gentle; they handled her like she was a priceless artefact.

"No," she shook her head slightly. "It was more the shock than anything."

"Here," Willow dropped one hand from her face, took her arm, and hauled her to her feet. Hazel couldn't help but stare. Compared to her average height and size, Willow dominated any space they were in. They were easily almost a foot taller than her, and their broad shoulders and muscled arms seemed to wrap around her, as if she was protected from everything just by being in their presence. Hazel noticed she'd been staring for some time, but she also noticed that Willow's hand was still resting on her cheek, their thumb working back and forth in tiny strokes. They also seemed incapable of looking away.

"You guys are sooooo precious!" a voice squealed and snapped them both out of their reverie.

I forgot she was here. Hazel cringed inwardly at her thought and shuffled awkwardly towards the reflection. Behind her, Willow cleared their throat and moved silently towards the kitchen, where they busied themselves by filling the kettle.

"Tea anyone?" they asked as the old faucet spluttered and splashed.

"Please."

"Eww, no thank you."

Hazel and the reflection exchanged surprised looks at their simultaneous answers.

"You don't like tea?" Hazel questioned.

"Nope," the reflection answered as she tried to hop up onto the kitchen table. She was halfway up when one of her arms gave out and she almost tumbled to the floor again. She managed to catch herself, but Hazel and Willow exchanged slightly bemused looks. The reflection continued on as if she hadn't just embarrassed herself.

"I like coffee... Black with no sugar. Hey, isn't this fun? New places, new memories, gah, I just love it."

Hazel was dumbfounded. Coffee? New places? No sugar?! Something had indeed gone terribly wrong with her spell if even the screw-up was *this* screwed up.

"Hang on," she started with a heavy sigh and rubbed at her temples. "You're my reflection—" the reflection nodded enthusiastically. "You're *my* reflection, so... so you're me, right?"

"Umm, yeah... no," the reflection replied happily as she picked up a spell book and flipped through it. Hazel rolled her eyes as a page managed to get torn.

"I'm confused," she said as she snatched the book away. "Explain to me how you're me, but not me."

"Well, I don't really know how you did it, but you brought me to life. I'm separate from you now. But I'm your reflection, like you said, because you're so smart, you see, you figured that out straight away. Not like me. I'm a total moron. I'd have been here for days wondering what the hell I'd done and getting nowhere. Oh, my—"

Hazel held up a hand and cut her off. This was going to get them nowhere.

"Please," she sounded as tired as she was starting to feel. "Please, just stick to the facts."

"Right, I can do that, no problem-o Hazel-o," the reflection shot a pair of finger guns at her. From the kitchen counter, Willow snorted and snickered into their hand, tea abandoned and long forgotten.

"The fact is that I'm you, but reflected. I'm your reflection after all, so everything is... umm... backwards? I guess that's the best word for it. I'm flipped, like in the mirror."

Confused silence fell in the cottage. The windows still rattled, and Hazel could hear the roof slates shifting above them. She'd have to ask Willow to check they hadn't lost any once the wind died down. As this thought occurred to her, she watched as Willow rounded the kitchen table and came to stand right in front of her. They took her by the shoulders and manoeuvred her to stand next to the reflection, and then they stooped slightly so they were at eye level with the two women. For a while, no one said anything; the pair just watched as Willow studied each of their faces closely, until eventually, their hand dropped from their chin and they smiled.

"She's right. She's a flipped version of you. I wonder..."

Hazel looked closely at the reflection while Willow politely asked her to take a seat at the kitchen table. They pulled out one of the rickety wooden chairs and sat the reflection down, then turned and did the same thing to Hazel. Hazel took in the face of her reflection. It looked identical to hers, as far as she could tell, but there was something almost... off about it. Something that didn't quite seem like she was looking at herself. She thought about how she looked in a mirror. The dark freckle under her left eye, the slight left-leaning curve of her small nose (which she was grateful to have back after last week), the way her right eye squinted slightly more and had more lines around it when she smiled. It was all there, but it was all on the other side, she realised. If the reflection smiled widely now, it would be her left eye that became slightly smaller. Her nose favoured the right, and the freckle was under her right eye.

The sound of another chair scraping the stone floor broke her from her thoughts, and she glanced at Willow, who was looking between them with a glint in their dark eyes.

"Let's see how far this goes," they said cryptically, and then turned towards the reflection, who beamed at them with a toothy smile.

My crooked right incisor is on her left, Hazel noticed.

"Do you have a name?" Hazel suddenly wondered aloud.

The reflection thought for a moment and then shrugged.

"Nope, I'm just your reflection. I'm you... essentially."

"Well, we can't call you both Hazel or it'll get confusing," Willow mused as they placed their chin in their hand. "What about Fawn? It's a synonym of Hazel."

The two women looked at each other and shrugged and nodded non-committedly. Fawn it was, since they had no better ideas.

"Ok, Fawn," Willow started again. "Answer this for me—what's your favourite food?"

"Cheese!" Fawn exclaimed.

I'm lactose intolerant, Hazel thought with a blanch.

"Favourite spell?"

"I don't use spells. My magic is strong enough that I don't need them."

Lucky cow.

"Introvert or extrovert?" Willow continued.

"Extrovert!"

Good lord, she's nothing like me!

"Who am I?"

Fawn shot a quizzical look at Hazel, who was staring incredulously back at her and wondering how the hell she'd ended up creating a reflection of herself like *this.*

"W–Willow?"

Willow nodded encouragingly, their hair bouncing slightly with the movement. Hazel was momentarily distracted by how soft their hair looked. In the decade since they'd met, she'd wanted to touch their hair countless times, but it never happened. Willow probably never noticed.

"And who am I to you, Fawn?"

Now Hazel was sure Willow was up to something. They were trying to see if everything Fawn said was the exact opposite of the answers Hazel would've given, but this question seemed loaded, and Hazel didn't want to hear the answer.

"You're like a sibling to me," Fawn answered quietly, but her tone indicated she thought the answer should be obvious.

Oh no, the opposite of someone 'being like a sibling' to you is...

"Yes... I... am," Willow said with a wry smile as they turned slowly to look at Hazel. She panicked and looked down, but not before catching the small wink they sent her way.

"One last question, Fawn, otherwise I won't be able to sleep tonight. What is your witch philosophy?"

The air around Hazel seemed to vanish. Of course, if everything was the opposite, then this would be, too. A witch's philosophy was the guiding force of how they lived their life and what they did with their time. There were three philosophies witches chose from: the betterment of mankind; the advancement of witchcraft; and the protection of nature. Hazel's philosophy was the protection of nature, and the opposite of that was...

"The destruction of nature," the reflection supplied with an innocent smile.

Oh.

Willow and Hazel shared a worried look, while Fawn merely leaned back in her chair and rocked it back onto the two rear legs with a passive smile.

"So we should..." Hazel began and waved her hand vaguely to fill in the blank.

"Right, but then what about...?" Willow supplied.

In her peripheral vision, Hazel watched as Fawn almost tipped right back in her chair. Her hand shot out and grasped the table edge to steady herself, and her eyes widened at the near miss.

Idiot.

"Well, we could always..."

"I don't know about that, Haze. What if...?"

"You're right." Hazel thought for a while.

In a flash, she was on her feet. The sudden commotion startled Fawn, who gasped and then suddenly, with an almighty crash, she was gone from Hazel's sight.

A groan sounded from the floor, along with some shuffling and the muted jangle of broken wood. Willow leaned over towards Hazel and whispered, "She doesn't seem like she has the brains to actually destroy anything, right?"

Hazel shot them a withering glare and rounded the table. The sight of Fawn on the cold stone floor, surrounded by bits of broken chair barely registered with her before she hauled Fawn to her feet with a clipped, "Come on. Up you get."

"Ooh, you're strong too! Not as strong as Willow, obviously, because... I mean, well, you know. But still pretty... Hey where are we going?"

Hazel tried to ignore the sound of Willow snickering again, and instead pushed Fawn towards the mirror. She had to admit, the girl could *talk*, and it seemed like she didn't have a bad bone in her body; but she was the direct opposite of Hazel herself. Fawn's philosophy meant that she could destroy everything Hazel worked to protect.

"It's been really great meeting you, but we just can't have someone with a destructive philosophy here, so..."

Fawn dug her heels into the floor with a rapid shaking of her head and an emphatic, "No, no, no, no, no! Please don't put me back in the mirror! I promise I won't do anything bad!"

Hazel and Fawn fought for dominance. One pushed on the other's shoulders in an attempt to get her to move towards the mirror. The other leant all her weight backwards and grappled onto the edge of the kitchen table in an attempt to stop her forward march. After a few more moments of struggle, Fawn seemed to be tiring, and Hazel felt confident in her victory.

"I'm glad you se—"

Fawn collapsed on the floor like a dead weight. Her backside hit the stone and her arms crossed as her entire face contorted into a pout.

"Are you... throwing a tantrum right now?!" Hazel scoffed, once again ignoring the muffled laughter coming from Willow, who had watched the entire situation unfold with a hand clamped over their mouth. But their eyes were practically sparkling with amusement.

"You can't make me," Fawn huffed. "I promise not to do anything bad. I'm not destructive, I swear!"

Hazel looked around her cottage. The side table lying on the floor, surrounded by now broken candles and smashed glass, and the broken chair lying by the kitchen table were evidence enough of Fawn's destruction, and that was all accidental. In a last-ditch attempt at handling the situation, Hazel did the one thing she always did when she was stuck with something. She turned to Willow.

"Oh no, no," they laughed as they registered the helpless look on Hazel's face. "You created her, you deal with it. This is *so* far above my pay grade."

"Please, Willow," Hazel whined with her best doe-eyed look.

Willow seemed to get lost in Hazel's wide eyes, their face embarking on a journey of a thousand emotions ranging from amused to determined, all the way through to helpless and weak. They just opened their mouth to reply, no doubt to give in, when Fawn's head popped up just in front of Hazel and peeked over the edge of the table.

"Yeah, please Willow?" She also adopted a 'lost puppy' expression that had Willow's gaze flitting from one woman to the other, seemingly completely confused now. Hazel elbowed Fawn in the back of the head.

"Don't *you* ask them for favours! They're my familiar!"

"Shush, I'm busy," Fawn hissed as she shot a rather angry glare over her shoulder and up at Hazel. She then turned her face back to Willow and resumed silently begging for their intervention.

"No, you shush," Hazel retorted as she stepped in front of Fawn's very effective begging face.

Fawn slapped Hazel on the back of her knee, causing it to buckle.

"Are you kidding me?!" Hazel grumbled as her hands shot out to steady herself against the table.

Before Willow knew what was happening, Hazel and Fawn were in an all-out slapping war. They watched as Hazel and her reflection, of all things, slapped each other's arms, backs, and legs, all the while arguing in tense growls about who Willow should help. If Hazel had been on the outside looking in, she would've been very unimpressed with the lack of maturity displayed. She wasn't though, was she? Nope, she was in the thick of it, repeatedly slapping her own reflection on the backside, since Fawn now had her in some odd pseudo-headlock.

"They're my familiar, Fawn!" Hazel's voice was a little muffled as she tried to pry herself away from Fawn's grip.

"Yeah, well, they're like my sibling, so they're—ow!—closer to me!"

"I was here first!"

"So what?!"

"So they're closer to me! I l—"

Suddenly Hazel stopped, frozen by the notion of what she was about to say. Awkward silence fell over the three, and Fawn very slowly released Hazel from her headlock. Hazel couldn't meet Willow's eyes, which she could feel burning into the top of her head as she looked down at her feet and prayed the ground would swallow her up. Fawn cleared her throat. Repeatedly.

"Maybe I would rather go back in the mirror," she said quietly. Hazel threw her a light elbow to the ribs and a glare. Fawn started to laugh as she stepped aside to avoid another one of Hazel's elbows. Her booted foot made contact with one of the candles she'd knocked off the side table earlier, and she slipped. Before she could fall and probably crack her skull on the stone floor, a hand shot out and grabbed her wrist. Hazel pulled her up to standing again with a reluctant twitch of her lips.

"Umm, ok, well, I think we should give her a chance to stay, Haze," Willow said as they watched the small exchange with a hopeful smile. Hazel still wouldn't meet their eyes, and instead chose to watch Fawn with an intense stare.

"If I let you stay, we have to have some ground rules," she said firmly.

Fawn nodded, and a small grin formed on her face.

"No unsupervised magic."

Fawn nodded again, the grin growing.

"No touching my spell books."

More nodding, more smiling.

"No puppy eyes at Willow."

Less enthusiastic nodding, grin faltering slightly.

"And you," Hazel turned on Willow, and their eyes widened in surprise. Why were they being given rules? "No caving in if she gives you puppy eyes."

Willow couldn't help but laugh as they stepped closer to Hazel, slung a heavy arm about her shoulders and gave her a little squeeze.

"It's not the puppy eyes that have me caving in, but sure," they said with a wink towards Fawn, who chuckled lightly in response. Hazel was lost, but it didn't seem like either of the others wanted to let her in on the joke.

"This is going to be great, guys!" Fawn exclaimed as she clapped her hands and bounced on her toes. "I promise to do my share of housework and I won't do anything destructive, and I'll make treats for us all the time. Oh, it'll be so much fun! Like a sleepover, except I've never had a sleepover, you know, since I'm new here. Like new as in just started existing today..."

She trailed off, just chattering away about sleepovers and making them a celebratory hot drink as she bounced towards the kitchen counters. Willow and Hazel exchanged a look.

"Well, I guess we have a new roommate, huh?" Willow asked with a smile.

"Ugh, you're enjoying this way too much."

"Just smile and nod Haze, it'll be fine. I promise."

There was a loud, metallic crunch from the kitchen and then the sound of rain got louder. Willow and Hazel looked over at Fawn, only to find her standing at the sink, kettle in one hand and the handle of the faucet in the other. Water sprayed from the tap with enough force to cover both her and the kitchen in heavy droplets.

Fawn shot them both an apologetic grimace and shrugged as if she had no idea what had happened.

"Oops."

Olivia Merchiston

OLIVIA MERCHISTON IS a writer, procrastinator, and freelancer. She lives on a tiny Scottish island with her very patient partner and very spoiled cat. When she isn't writing or working, she enjoys photography, videography, knitting and reading. A firm believer that there's a little magic in every life, Olivia is spending her thirties finding hers.

The Fourth Spire

by A. E. Lanier

He arrives to the acrid smell of burning, the five spires already in flames. Three of the towers have fallen, two still stand. The one nearest him is upright, but precarious. Its rough stones seem tired, on the verge of giving in. An angry, warm glow lurks behind some of the windows. But not all of them. Not yet.

The Great Burning lasted for over six hours, but it is near the end now. Much has already been lost. The texts here were carefully protected, the spires warded to prevent tampering. In the end, the very steps taken to protect the library condemned it. Enchantments kept rescuers from approaching once the fire started, both during the crisis and in the centuries that followed.

Yet here he stands on the edge of the greatest collection of knowledge ever gathered. He has found a loophole: a way in. Research has revealed that the wards weakened after the third tower fell. They did not fail entirely–some protections linger even in his own age. But he has begun to believe in a narrow window of time, after the fall of the third tower and before the library crumbles entirely to ash, where a skilled practitioner could enter the spires and bring something out.

Now, he is proven correct. He has traveled back to the last moments when the spires stood, has entered his own personal pocket of time. It is both a necessary part of the enchantment and a boon. Minutes will turn to hours, protecting him from sudden dangers and giving him space to work.

The excitement of the moment almost overwhelms him. He has thought of the spires every day since he learned of them as a child. Generations of knowledge, lost to caution and poor timing. A terrible tragedy which can now be repaired. He has no particular goal in mind because even that would limit the possibilities. The wonder and sorrow of this place have always been with him. It is not a thing he can fully understand, let alone explain.

Entry has been rockier than expected. His supplies have not made the journey with him and he is not entirely certain how he will transport things back. But no matter. He has made it this far, will succeed. Must. Any lingering fears that he has missed something are best ignored. This enchantment can only work once; there is no time to waste on uncertainty.

He stands for a moment, eyeing the two towers that still stand, the ruins of the fallen three. He breathes in the thick smoke, which pools sluggishly in the air and in his lungs. The streets are empty. The people of this place will not appear in his created pocket of time, although he imagines keepers frantically rushing around the remaining towers. Not everything was lost in the Burning, just most things. Less now, if he is successful.

The stones beneath his feet are small and smooth. Cobbles, but strange ones. This is the Azure Courtyard, another name out of legend and myth that always seemed strange and now becomes clear. The stones are unlike any he has ever seen: each a rich, gleaming blue. After the final spire falls, the fire will grow more intense, the heat enough to crack these stones open. Their remains will linger for centuries, cracked and gray. All beauty and luster forgotten.

He had not thought of saving the courtyard itself and has no way of doing so, yet suddenly he longs to. A strange sorrow overwhelms him and he struggles to push it back. He is here for books, not stones. He pauses, caresses one of the blue cobbles with his left hand. It comes away blackened with ash.

He has spent many years searching for a way to travel back to this place; does not have time to be overwhelmed by sentimentality. So he turns away from the cobbles, towards the fourth spire. It will be the last to fall, and he is here to save what he can.

The tower is like something out of a children's tale. Of all the spires, only the fourth's walls are perfectly smooth. Cream and glittering even now, when surrounded by ash and smoke. The great wooden doorway is wondrous, its intricate runes exactly as he'd imagined. Soon they will be devoured by flame, lost to all but fading memory.

He is here to save, not to mourn. Stumbles inside. The spire seems empty and might be so in truth. Little from the fourth spire was saved. The library was understaffed when the Burning began and became more so as its keepers went to find help. A quirk of the flame-fused wards prevented those who left from returning. By the time the Great Burning ends, the spires left in rubble and ash, there will be no one left to witness it.

The entryway of the spire opens into a round reception area. The fire is already here, although it does not appear to have spread beyond this room. Perhaps the wards of the fourth spire are superior to those of the other towers. The flames move sluggishly, so slowly it is difficult to tell they are moving at all. The heat is palpable, but there is little danger for him here. Time moves so slowly in his pocket of enchantment that it is unlikely flame or falling rubble will surprise him.

A great polished desk waits in the center of the room to direct visitors. It is carefully made, but flames eat at the detailed carving on its legs and edges. The fire is unnatural: a color he cannot name, which is off-putting. He looks away, quashing the impulse to put the fire out. Any attempt will both fail and waste time.

Staircases spiral up from the edges of the room, leading into the collection. Each is different: one of iron, one of polished marble, one of the same smooth cream the tower itself is made of. He does not know what the staircases signify. There is no record of them. He chooses the closest and climbs, tries not to think.

The air is thick with the smell of ash and burning paper, but there is not yet enough smoke in the fourth tower to be a problem. At last, the stairs deposit him on a vast, round floor and he pauses, awestruck once again.

It is exactly what he imagined as a child. Scrolls rest gently in their cradles; tomes wait patiently on great wooden shelves. Whole civilizations preserved in parchment and vellum. He cannot save even a fraction of a fraction of what is here. He does not even know the cataloging system. But no matter. This is the beginning of a larger project. His enchantment is replicable; his work was a beginning, not an end. Others will follow.

He moves, trance-like, towards a shelf of dark oak and reaches for a thin, clothbound volume. It does not matter what it holds; everything here is worth saving. He tries to grab the book. Fails. Like a ghost in a children's tale, he can feel the soft roughness of the cloth but cannot fully touch it. The book will not move.

The apprehension he has ignored until now overwhelms him. He could try again, perhaps ought to, but he knows with a terrible certainty that it is futile. Whether through some failing of his own enchantment or a twisted success of the wards, he can touch nothing in the library. He is not the beginning of a new age of discovery, but one in a long line of mages who foolishly believed that he could succeed where others had failed.

The tatters of his confidence fade and he falls to his knees, eyes clouded with tears he had not anticipated. He is not a child. He has seen much in his time: traveled far through time and space, faced great cruelty, great injustice. But, somehow, this is different, worse. The senselessness of the Great Burning overwhelms him. He cannot stand, cannot begin to imagine how it might be done.

A loud crack issues from outside, lingering terribly in his disconnected mind. The second spire has given in. Will fall over protracted minutes. This spire is next. No matter.

"Oh, another one of you. I thought I might have found the last already."

He looks up to see a young woman. She is dressed like one of the keepers of this place, her pale robes streaked with soot. A librarian and a great mage in her own right, as she has managed to enter his pocket of time.

The enchantment that allows him to understand her is a simple thing, effortless. The spoken word is easily translated, although marks on the page are much harder to shift. He wonders how many languages are present in this spire alone. He'll never know.

"Come on then," her voice is kind but firm. He does not move. None of this is what he expected. She takes his hand, pulls him to his feet. He blinks at her uncertainly, still numb with failure. The confidence of this morning a distant memory.

The keeper pauses, takes the book bound in blue cloth he had reached for earlier and hands it to him. He clutches it to his chest like a child, finds the book makes him feel somehow more solid. He knows the feeling is entirely imagined, is grateful for it all the same.

Somehow she has overcome the wards, allowed him to interact physically with this place. He wonders if it is the same magics that enabled her to enter his pocket of time. Perhaps she can explain it to him. Perhaps the enchantment is replicable.

She sees the longing in his face, recognizes it instantly. "It won't work. We've tried. I can hand them to you, but carrying them out is a different story. The wards might overlook one if you bury it deep in your coat. More than that and they start to see the pattern. Still, even this much would have been impossible before the third tower fell. You were very clever, making it this far."

She says it kindly, and he has the terrible feeling that she has had this conversation many times before. He grips the book harder, and the keeper nods encouragingly.

"You all seem happier when you can keep one."

"What is it?" His voice is hoarse and not from the smoke.

She shrugs. "I can't read any of the languages in the fourth spire. But it's yours now. It's time to go."

She sets off down the twisting staircase and he follows her, half-awake. She waits for him in the Azure Courtyard, gaze lingering sadly on the cobbles, as if she knows what's coming next. As if she, too, regrets the stones as much as the books.

"Come on then," her voice is kind but firm. "If I leave you here, you'll just find some corner to stand in and eventually burn to death."

He is embarrassed to realize she is probably right, which is a shamefully dramatic response. But then, he has worked for this all his life, has failed.

She makes her way carefully across the courtyard, and he follows. The second spire has nearly finished falling, the last of its rough stones rolling slowly away. The top of the tower lies in pieces, exhausted walls jutting painfully up into the orange sky. The inside must be a furnace by now. Everything lost.

She takes him by the arm and leads him through the burning rubble of her life's work. He is still crying, but her eyes are clear. They leave the library and come to a meadow, a ring of stones. The place where he arrived from.

She walks him to the edge of the circle but does not step inside. She is no fool.

"Don't feel bad," her voice is kind, not patronizing. "People like you will always find their way here. The kind of person who would come, raised with the kind of power to make this sort of travel possible, can never bear to watch it happen."

"How do you stand it?" His voice breaks. He hugs his book closer.

She smiles, sadly but sincerely. "Knowledge is always lost. There will be more."

Smoke billows up from the greatest library in the world, filling the sky. Soon, it will burn hot enough to break even the cobbles underfoot.

"Not knowledge like this."

She looks at him pityingly. "That is always true. Of every life, as much as every book or scroll. But that is hard for your kind to understand. You grow up in a way where death remains, but every scroll has a thousand copies. And so, you understand war, but not the burning of libraries."

He realizes she is correct, is embarrassed to have been seen so clearly. Embarrassed, too, that this woman knew he would fail before he did.

"You may be the last," she sounds almost wistful. "It has been a long time since I've found one of you. And then I suppose we both have to figure out what comes next."

He feels, suddenly, that to linger would be wrong. This woman may be stronger than him, but she is still losing everything. She has her own grief, does not need to carry his. He steps into the circle and turns to face her. There is ash on her face and on her hands.

"What is your name?"

She smiles, like he is finally paying attention. Speaks her name, melodic and bright and unlike any he has heard.

He repeats it, the strange syllables tripping unfamiliarly, alive all the same. "Thank you. And I'm sorry."

She nods, and he sees his own sorrow mirrored back in her face. Better controlled, there nonetheless. She turns and heads back to her spires. Soon, they will be nothing but dust.

He has taken a name and a single book he will not be able to read. It is something.

A. E. Lanier

A. E. LANIER IS A WRITER, educator, and chronic overthinker living in Central Texas. She enjoys caves, silent reading, and other people's cats. Her work has appeared in *The Arcanist* and *Daily Science Fiction.*

The War Babies

By Roberta Eaton Cheadle

1 November 1916

The three women stood on the platform. The train had long since disappeared into the heavy mist, but still they stood, staring at the empty tracks.

The eldest of the three, a middle-aged woman wearing sensible lace-up shoes, a heavy winter coat, and a plain hat pulled down low over her greying hair, sighed deeply and looked away.

"Come on girls," she said, false cheerfulness giving her voice a tinny edge. "Let's find a café and get a cuppa. A hot drink will do us the world of good, and a slice of apple pie wouldn't go amiss either."

The two younger women nodded. Tears leaked from the eyes of the shorter of the pair and ran in unchecked rivulets down her cheeks.

"Come on Lizzie," the taller woman looped her arm through her sister's. "Mum's right. A piping hot cuppa will go down a treat, and I'm starving." She patted the bulge of her pregnant stomach.

As the three walked away, the yellow tinge to the taller woman's skin was jarring in comparison to the doughy complexion of her mother and pink and white prettiness of her sister.

Fifteen minutes later, the trio entered a small tearoom and seated themselves at a table for four near a large window.

Another gusty sigh escaped from the older woman's thin-lipped mouth. "I'm glad to rest my feet," she said.

"I saw they're quite swollen again, Mum," said the yellow-skinned woman.

"I've been soaking them in a cool Epsom salt bath, Mol," her mother replied. "It helps with the swelling. You should get some for later," she nodded significantly towards Molly's bump, "Your feet will swell towards the end." She paused, readying herself for the kill. "Especially if you continue in your current job."

The tired-looking waitress came over and took their orders, relieving Mol of the duty of responding to her mother's comment.

Mol reached over and swirled her hand in a circle on the window. A peep hole appeared in the condensation, obscured by raindrops. She watched the shadowy shapes of people hurrying past on the street outside. Her mother's words were not lost on her, neither was her gesture towards Mol's swollen belly and not Lizzie's, even though both of their babies were due less than a month apart.

Mum gave their orders. "Three teas and three apple pies with custard."

The waitress shuffled away, and her mum looked at Mol expectantly.

Why can't she just drop it, Mol thought, rolling her eyes.

"I like my job, Mum," she said, cringing internally at the defensiveness in her voice. "And it is important work for the war. The government needs munitions workers."

"But look at you, Mol. You are yellow!"

Mrs Vera Stubbs leaned down and pulled a small, stained hand mirror from her cavernous bag. She held it in front of Mol's face.

Mol's reflection stared back at her in accusation. Her skin was the bright yellow of a canary, hence the nickname of 'canary girls' assigned to the munitions girls. A fuzz of short, crinkly ginger hair decorated her forehead and stood up on her crown.

I look hideous. Like a circus freak.

Pushing the mirror away, she said: "The job's well paid and I'm doing vital war work. Jimmy's proud of me."

"Jimmy," her mum snorted. "He ain't here, is he? And he may never be. He's gone back to the front and left you to bring up the kid alone."

Vera broke off in mid-rant.

Tears ran unchecked down her younger daughter's face, splashing onto her protruding stomach.

Reaching out, Vera patted Lizzie's hand. "There, there, Lizzie, don't cry. Will and Jimmy will both be back, mark my words."

"The storks are bringing you and Mol war babies," she smiled. "Do you remember that story? About the storks? You loved it as a girl, and Mol used to read it to you."

The weary waitress rattled over carrying a tray laden with a fat teapot, three teacups and saucers, and three delectable slices of steaming apple pie smothered in thick custard.

Glancing at Lizzie's tear-stained face, she dumped the items on the table and waddled off as quickly as possible.

Mum poured the tea and added sugar and milk to each cup. She continued to distract Lizzie with talk of her favourite girlhood story.

Mol's mind wandered.

"The Storks" was not a pleasant story, she thought. *The storks punished the naughty boy who teased them by bringing his mother a stillborn baby. The war is like the storks. It has brought many women babies, some unwanted. But mine is wanted. My Jimmy is delighted we are having a child, and he's fighting to ensure our future safety.*

Lots of the canary girls have had babies and they've all been fine. They're born yellow, that's true, but the colour fades with time.

Mol jutted out her chin defiantly. *I'm going to keep doing my duty, and I'll work at the factory until the baby comes at the end of January.*

Her decision reaffirmed, Mol turned her attention to the apple pie.

"Oh my," she said, swallowing a mouthful. "This really hits the spot."

28 DECEMBER 1916

Mol stood in the changing room in her underwear.

"You'll have to take that off," the supervisor pointed at her bra. "It's got a metal clip."

Nodding, Mol removed the offending article and dressed in her extra-large boiler suit. Around her, other girls were changing and removing any banned items of clothing.

Clothing made from silk, hair grips, and anything containing metal had to be removed.

"A rogue spark caused by static could cause an explosion," the supervisor had explained. "We definitely do not want that."

The women obliged cheerfully; they knew their work was dangerous.

"Give me a hand with my boots, Sarah," Mol asked the woman changing next to her.

At nearly eight-months pregnant, Mol could no longer bend over and pull on the compulsory gumboots.

Ten minutes later, the women had clocked in and were seated at work benches in the workroom. Wearing masks, they set about the demanding task of filling the shell casings with powder, putting a detonator in the top and then, gently, tapping it down. The work required concentration and little talking took place during work sessions. The women made up for this silence during their breaks in the canteen, when raucous laughter and a ceaseless flow of chatter helped relieve the tension.

KABAM!

The explosion rocked the tables and work benches. There was silence, followed by a terrible screaming.

MOL WOKE TO A SILENT, white world. Every part of her hurt and her head ached violently.

Looking down, she saw her body was flat beneath the sheets.

"My baby," her voice was a whisper.

A pale face topped by an even whiter cap floated above her. "Your baby's fine. He's small, but his lungs are strong. The doctor had to do a Caesarean operation. Now rest, and don't talk."

Mol's eyes fluttered closed. She slept.

Some time later, a nurse brought her son to her. He was small, with a head that appeared too big for his scrawny body. He was also bright yellow. His colouring was not unexpected, but the sight of his puckered up, yellow face peeping out from the folds of the white hospital blanket startled Mol.

"He looks like an alien," she gasped.

The nurse was kind and helped Mol latch the baby, so that he could feed. Despite his bird-like appearance, he had a strong suck, and the nurse smiled.

"He's a strong boy. Don't worry about his yellowness, it will fade. What's his name?"

"Robert," the word scratched Mol's throat. She accepted a drink of water from the nurse and moaned at the pain caused by the slight movement.

The baby finished feeding, and the nurse laid him in a bassinet next to her bed. "Now rest," she said. "You need to recover from the surgery."

Mol drifted into a restless sleep, and the memory of the explosion at the factory surfaced.

She dreamed that an army of storks in uniforms were delivering babies to expectant mothers. The anti-aircraft guns boomed as they fired at the line of flying birds. The storks were singing the words of the ditty from the story her sister had loved so much.

"The third will be shot with a bang
The fourth will be roast for the squire."

IT WAS A FULL WEEK before Mol learned the details of what happened at the factory that day.

She was sitting up in bed, feeding Robert, who was always hungry, when one of her work colleagues walked into the ward.

"Hi Mol," said Evelyn.

Dragging a wooden stool over to Mol's bed, she plumped herself down. "My, it feels good to be off my feet."

Mol smiled at the words, so reminiscent of her mum.

Evelyn reached into her handbag and retrieved a package. She handed it to Mol. "My Beth made these for you."

Inside the package was a selection of homemade shortbread.

"What a wonderful gift, Evelyn. Please thank your daughter for me. Here, try one?"

Evelyn took the offered biscuit, and they both sat, quietly munching.

"This is the best shortbread I've ever tasted," Mol exclaimed.

Smiling with pleasure, Evelyn told Mol that Beth had a 'light touch' with baking and produced the most delicious biscuits and cakes. "Mr Groves has offered her a position working in his bakery on Saturday and Sunday. Of course, she jumped at the chance."

"What a wonderful opportunity for her," Mol said.

Mol felt Evelyn's eyes inspecting her. "I must admit," her visitor said, "you look good. I thought it would take longer for you to recover from a Caesarean operation."

"Thank you, Evelyn. My incision has healed nicely, and I'm expecting to go home soon."

"What! Going home a week after a Caesarean operation?" Evelyn was shocked. "I suppose they want the bed."

Evelyn shook her head in bewilderment, and then looked at the bassinet next to Mol. "How's the baby?"

"He's doing well," said Mol. "He's so hungry, I'm having to top him up with milk from a bottle."

"I'm happy to hear that. It is a blessing that everything turned out well for the two of you." The corners of Evelyn's mouth curled down in an expression of sorrow.

"I don't know what happened at the factory last week, Evelyn. I can remember the explosion, but that's all." Mol looked at her friend with anxious expectation.

Evelyn glanced around furtively. Seeing the nurse was nowhere near, she leaned towards Mol and whispered, "Sarah was badly injured in the blast. It seems she tapped the detonator too hard when she inserted it into the shell casing, and it went off. The explosion flung all the women at her table across the room. You and Alice were knocked out and ended up in the hospital. The rest of us were just battered and bruised."

Evelyn rolled up the sleeve of her left arm and showed Mol the huge greeny-yellow bruise that ran all the way up her arm."

"I fell on my arm and leg," she said.

"That looks painful." Mol's face had paled.

"Aww, it's not that bad." Evelyn grinned wickedly. "You should see my arse and thigh. I'd show you, but the nurse might come back, and we don't need her stomping and shrieking all over the place."

Mol laughed and then pulled a wry face. "My being knocked out explains why I can't remember what happened, and why I've been getting such bad headaches. The pain is here." Moll cupped the area at the back of her head, just above her neck. "The doctor said I mustn't knit, read, or sew, for another five weeks, and I must avoid bright light."

Evelyn nodded in understanding. "You have a concussion."

Mol dropped her voice conspiratorially. "Is Sarah recovering?"

"The doctor says she'll recover, but the blast blinded her, and she's lost both her hands."

Mol's face drained of colour just as the nurse bustled through the door.

"Visiting hours are over," she announced. "All visitors need to please leave."

There was a flurry of activity as visitors stood, pulled on their coats, and said goodbye to friends and loved ones.

Evelyn reached for her bag and struggled to her feet. "Goodbye, Mol. I'm glad you and Robert are doing well. I'll pop by for a cuppa once you are back home."

Mol slept poorly that night. In her dream, she was trying to tend to Robert, but she was blind and had no hands. Mum took the baby from her arms to bathe him. "I told you to leave your job, but you wouldn't listen. Now look where your misguided loyalty has landed you. You have a baby and no way of looking after him or making a living in the future."

Outside the windows, Mol could hear the storks in uniform singing their mocking song:

"The first little stork they will hang

The second will fry by the fire."

What does it mean? Is my baby going to die? Am I being punished for some perceived lack of care with my work?

31 JANUARY 1917

Lizzie's baby was born naturally four weeks after Mol returned home.

Elsie was a beautiful child with pink cheeks, a fluff of white hair, and screw-on hands and feet.

When the two new mothers bathed their babies in the old tin washtub in front of the fire, Robert looked yellower than ever in comparison to the rose pink and white of his cousin.

Elsie was an easy baby and cooed contentedly, bringing up her wind easily and only crying when she was hungry.

Robert fretted and cried all day and all night. There was little reprieve for Mol, who was exhausted from the lack of sleep and relentlessness of seeing to her son's needs.

"He's colicky," Mum said, handing the howling child back to Mol.

Mum's eyes held the silent judgement that Mol had brought this on herself by working at the factory.

During low moments when Robert cried unconsolably, Mol would sit in her chair, gently rocking him. Memories of newspaper stories she'd read about desperate new mothers who resorted to injuring their screaming babies filled her troubled mind.

I can sympathise with their desperation. Nothing you do stops the endless crying; it goes on and on. Combined with the lack of sleep, it wears you down and shatters your nerves.

She reflected on Mum's unheeded warnings about her job not being suitable for an expectant mother, and guilt consumed her.

If I hadn't insisted on continuing to work at the factory, Robert wouldn't have been born early and he wouldn't be yellow.

Any short periods of sleep between Robert's fits of crying were disturbed by the army of vengeful storks in uniforms who haunted her dreams. She would wake, panicked, and soaked in sweat, clutching the sheets to her chest in the dazed belief they were her crying baby.

16 FEBRUARY 1917

Mol sat at the kitchen table, trying valiantly to drink a cup of tea laced with whisky. The comforting liquid could not pass the constriction in her throat and, after spluttering and choking over a few sips, she left it to grow cold.

Lizzie and Mum had taken the two babies out in the pram, leaving her to digest the content of the telegram that lay, crumpled, on the table next to the discarded tea.

Jimmy's dead! Dead of wounds at a Casualty Clearing Station three days ago.

Mum's words of consolation had barely penetrated the loud clashing of her wayward thoughts. "I'm so sorry, Love ... died a brave death ... a hero ..."

The look of desperate relief on Lizzie's face made her stomach heave.

A sound like distant machine gun fire buzzed in Mol's head. Closing her eyes, and dropping her head into her cupped hands, she visualised a stork, its bill opening and closing rapidly to produce the noisy knocking sound.

23 MARCH 1917

The two women stood in the graveyard. Their fellow mourners had long since disappeared to the local pub, but still they stood, staring at the plain, wooden coffin in the hole.

Later, the gravedigger would return and cover it up with hard, dark earth. In the spring, the resultant mound would be sewn with grass, and a headstone would be planted bearing the words "Margaret (Molly) Harris - 17 September 1894 to 20 March 1917.

The dark grey sky started spitting snowflakes, which settled momentarily on the scarves and shoulders of the two women, before melting into damp patches.

"We better get going," Vera said to Lizzie, the words slurring through her numb lips. "It's freezing cold out here."

In the covered pram, a baby started to whimper.

Lifted the covering, Lizzie removed her glove and stroked the downy head of the little boy. "Poor little lad," she said. "He's lost his father and his mother within a month."

The two babies were lying head to toe and, after checking on her sleeping daughter, Lizzie pulled up the cover and wheeled the perambulator along the path towards the gate.

Her mother shuffled along behind her. The death of her oldest daughter had aged Vera. Her eyes were deeply sunken into bruised looking eye sockets and her body looked broken down.

Mol's demise had been unexpected and shockingly fast.

A week to the day after the arrival of the telegram informing them of the death of Jimmy Harris, Mol had woken with a headache, nausea, and intermittent abdominal pain.

"It feels like my head's being squeezed in a vice," she'd moaned.

Over the course of the next week, Mol's symptoms worsened. She slept for long periods. Her face grew thinner and yellower, gradually taking on a strange transparency through which the blue veins of her forehead plainly showed.

Dr. Green made a home visit and diagnosed toxic jaundice.

"I'm seeing other similar cases among the munitions workers at the factory," he said. He prescribed a limited diet and a mixture of potassium citrate, neither of which made any difference to Mol's rapid decline.

During her increasingly rare periods of wakefulness, Mol complained that her mind was foggy, and she couldn't think.

Lizzie took over the care of Robert and Vera helped her move him onto cow's milk from a bottle, Mol being too weak to continue feeding her rapidly growing son.

When Lizzie laid the baby next to his mother so that she could inhale his sweet baby smell and stroke his little head, she was struck by the stark contrast between mother and child. Robert had lost his scrawny, premature baby look and was plump and bonny. His skin discolouration had faded to a pale yellow.

Mol looked at him with sad, wistful eyes tinged with yellow. "I'm dying, Lizzie," she said.

"Oh no, Mol, don't say that," Lizzie cried. "You must get well. Please, Mol, you have to keep fighting."

"I want to, Lizzie, I really want to, but every day I feel myself growing a little weaker and I know I shan't gain it back."

Mol stopped speaking and lay quietly on her pillow for several minutes. "Promise me you'll look after Robert, Lizzie. When I'm gone. Promise you'll be good to him."

"Of course I will, Mol. I promise you." Lizzie leaned into her sister and laid her plump pink and white cheek against Mol's shrivelled yellow one. "Don't worry, Dear One, I'll love Robert like my own son."

Two days later, Mol was dead.

The wind was bitter as Lizzie wheeled the pram up the steep hill towards home. Her mother stumbled along behind her, clutching her worn coat tightly to her chest.

They passed The White Stork, the local pub where many of the mourners were enjoying an ale and a plate of fish or pie and chips. The windows were opaque with condensation, and Lizzie could only see dark shapes moving around inside. One shadow had a strangely stork-like appearance and Lizzie thought about her favourite story, The Storks.

The Storks brought Mol and I our war babies and both are doing well. It seems they took Mol as recompense for her patriotism and devotion to the war.

A silent tear slipped down Lizzie's cheek. She took a deep breath and pressed on into the teeth of the wind.

Roberta Eaton Cheadle

ROBERTA EATON CHEADLE is a writer of young adult and adult fiction in the supernatural fantasy, historical horror, and historical supernatural genres. Under the name **Robbie Cheadle,** she is a South African children's author, publishing the Sir Chocolate series with her son, Michael, and a poet with 2 published poetry books.

To date, Roberta has published two novels, *Through the Nethergate*, and *A Ghost and His Gold*, along with several short stories in various anthologies including *Whispers of the Past*, *Spirit of the West*, and *Where Spirits Linger*, all edited and compiled by Kaye Lynne Booth, and *Dark Visions, Nightmareland, Spellbound*, *Wings & Fire*, and *Shadowland*, all compiled by Dan Alatorre.

Robbie is also a member of the *Writing to be Read* blogging team and co-editor of *Poetry Treasures* (2021) and *Poetry Treasures 2: Relationships* (2022), two poetry anthologies with contributing authors who were guests from her "Treasuring Poetry" blog series. When she is not writing, Robbie enjoys working in the garden and creating fondant and cake artworks to be featured in her children's books.

THE MIRROR SLACKED

By Rebecca M. Senese

THE MIRROR HUNG ON the stone wall of the palace, in an alcove just off the main throne room. It was the perfect spot to observe the proceedings, to admire the cream marble floor, laced with blue like delicate veins. Woven tapestries lined the wall opposite, made of the finest fabrics and weaves, depicting great battles and plentiful harvests.

Thick burgundy curtains, pulled back and tied with gold sashes, hung on either side of the alcove, delineating it from the throne room. A round basin, made of a rare, light grey stone polished smooth until it almost sparkled, rested on a table beneath the mirror, a pitcher of spring water beside it for anyone who wished to wash their hands or face before the mirror, but no one ever did. No one used the mirror to help cleanse themselves.

No, that would be too ordinary.

The mirror was a simple mirror, oval with a thin, black frame, nothing too ornate or gaudy. The king had inlaid it inside a different frame once, a hideous thing of gold that looked like flames shooting out around the mirror. It hated that look. That frame made the mirror look like it was some kind of all-seeing oracle in some third-rate circus.

In protest, the mirror turned black until the king removed the frame.

Which he promptly did.

So now the mirror sat with its simple black frame in an elegant alcove, observing the business of the realm. Petitions, judgments, complaints, admonishments. Citizens, delegations, officers, all came for an audience before the king. At times, it was interesting—other times not so much, but the mirror watched it all as witness.

And then came the day of the greatest excitement. The king's remarriage.

He had been wed before, to a lovely princess from another kingdom, but she had died in childbirth. The child, a beautiful girl with golden hair just like her father's, had grown to be a lovely young woman. The mirror had watched as she attended her father, learning the business of court. She even came to the mirror at times, brushing some stray speck of dust from her cheek, checking her hair, straightening her gown. The mirror was always happy to reflect her back to herself, her kind eyes, her intelligent gaze, her beauty and strength.

A lovely reflection.

And now, after so many years alone, the king had found a new bride.

The wedding was held in the throne room, giving the mirror a perfect view. The new queen wore a gown of shimmering silver, complimenting the king's uniform of navy and burgundy. A veil of lace and silver covered her face and hair, hiding her from view. If it could, the mirror would have quivered in anticipation. Seeing was everything to the mirror. Not being able to see the new queen filled it with an uneasy delight. Was she similar to the first queen with hair of spun gold and alabaster skin? The mirror couldn't wait to see.

The high priest of the religion droned on, his voice high and grating. The mirror never bothered to pay attention. Then the priest gestured at the king. The king lifted the veil, revealing the mirror's first glimpse of the new queen.

Her hair was as black as midnight, curled and coiled in a perfect sculpture atop her head. Her skin was the darkest brown, almost black, with a smooth sheen that glimmered against the silver of her dress. Her eyes were dark pools of mystery and when she smiled at the king, they twinkled in the light.

The king smiled back as he leaned in to kiss her.

If it could, the mirror would have swooned.

The celebration went well into the night, keeping even the mirror awake to all hours. Musicians played lively music. A buffet stretched the length of the throne, filled with all sorts of culinary delights, from the usual roast pork and roasted potatoes with vegetables, to such strange things as pastries woven into different shapes and filled with jams and fruits. People laughed and danced and ate, and in the center was the king with his new queen, dancing together, arms around each other as they gazed only upon the other as if they were the only two people in the room.

The mirror found it all terribly romantic.

Toward the end of the evening, the princess stole into the alcove. The mirror was so intent on watching the party that it didn't even notice her until her face filled its gaze. Dark shadows dimmed the light in her eyes. Her mouth, usually upturned in an almost constant smile, was now flat and straight in a line of dispassion.

She cleared her throat and spoke aloud.

"Mirror, mirror, on the wall, who is the fairest of them all?"

Such a question, in the middle of a wedding celebration? The princess, of course, was one of the fairest, but the bride certainly outshone her at the moment, if only as it was her wedding. But should the mirror mention that? After all, it could see that the princess was perhaps not so thrilled to have a new stepmother after so many years alone with her father.

It certainly must be difficult for the poor child.

So how to answer?

The mirror could take the question quite literally. Then the princess was indeed the fairest. She was certainly lighter than the queen with her dark completion. The mirror wouldn't be lying then.

"You are the fairest," the mirror intoned.

A self-satisfied smile curled the princess's lips. Too bad it created creases around her mouth that marred the perfection of her reflection. Not that she noticed, but the mirror did.

It was about to mention it when she spun and flounced away, kicking up the hem of her gown.

If the mirror breathed, it would have sighed.

AND SO, THE YEARS WENT by. The mirror enjoyed its view from the alcove, watching all the petitions and presentations to the king. As he grew older, the king shifted more and more on his throne. Not that the mirror could blame him. The throne was made of a dark, hard wood, polished and shining, but it didn't have any cushioning at all. Tradition held that it was to be sat upon as it was built, a single block of wood, carved into an elaborate throne, with armrests that curled forward and a seat, that although angled to cradle a rump, was still hard wood.

In between petitions, the king came into the alcove, using the basin and pitcher of water to wash his face to refresh himself. The mirror saw the white now mingling with his blond hair, the creases and lines that wrinkled his face, giving him a look of wisdom and patience.

But the mirror knew the king did not feel wise.

"What am I to do?" he would say. "My wife, the queen, and my daughter, the princess, do not get along. How am I to rule and spread peace through the land when I cannot bring peace to my own house?"

The mirror was willing to answer, but could not, as the king did not address these questions to it. He spoke to himself as he bent over the basin, never once lifting his eyes to his reflection. Without that direct look, the mirror could not respond.

There were strict rules about that sort of thing.

Then the king would wipe the water from his face, brush his hair back from his forehead and turn back to the throne, never speaking directly to the mirror, never letting it help him.

And what would the mirror have said?

It would have told him they fought because they were too much alike and yet very different. The princess feeling usurped, the queen feeling disrespected, so they fought to defend their position, not realizing that the main thing they had in common, loving the king, was the thing they were hurting with this feud.

It was enough to give the mirror a headache, if it had a head.

Because they kept dragging it into the middle.

First would come the princess. Her golden hair piled high on her head, tendrils of curls spilling to her shoulders, looking almost ethereal in a light blue gown with long sleeves trimmed in burgundy. She pressed her hands to the wood table on either side of the basin as she leaned forward to peer into the mirror.

"Mirror, mirror, who is the fairest?" she asked.

And the mirror would respond because of her alabaster skin. "You are the fairest."

Always it hoped she would ask another question, but always she smiled a smile that thinned her lips and made her eyes look cruel before she turned and walked away.

Then came the queen. After the wedding, she took to wearing gowns of dark burgundy, woven with silver thread that shimmered. Her black, curling hair that puffed out wider than her shoulders, she kept held back from her face with a silver headband. Her dark skin was smooth and unlined, even as the king's developed wrinkles, but she had the handsomeness of maturity in poise.

"Mirror, mirror, who is the fairest?" she would ask.

And the mirror would answer, because it had seen how she always tried to listen to both sides of a disagreement. How she helped steer the king's decisions, even if it meant inconvenience, but was fair to the other party. How she still insisted the king spend time with his daughter, even as the princess was curt and rude to her.

"You are the fairest," the mirror said.

The queen bowed her head and stepped away.

And so it went, the questions asked and answered as best as the mirror could reply. But it was not happy.

In fact, it was getting downright annoyed with both of them.

And after ten years of the same question, the mirror decided it had had enough.

THE NEXT MORNING DAWNED bright and sunny. Even in its alcove, the mirror could see the sunshine reflecting on the polished marble floor. The tapestries looked vivid, the images bold and vibrant. The mirror could almost see a glint on the silver fabric blade raised above a dragon's head or smell the bountiful wheat which appeared to almost sway across the tapestry.

Well, it would smell it if it had a nose.

But it could admire the greens and blues and reds and browns in the tapestries. The sunlight sparkling on the marble floor, highlighting the veins of blue. The sheen of the dark wood on the throne and the richness of the burgundy drapes lining the alcove.

A beautiful, perfect morning.

The mirror loved mornings like this.

The soft tap of a step sounded and drew closer. It was very early. Perhaps it was one of the cleaners, come to inspect the mirror. They did that from time to time, expecting to need to dust it, but the mirror was always clean. Dust did not adhere to it, even if there had been any dust around. But the maids were so diligent, not even a speck of dust appeared in the throne room.

The mirror always thought it was an excuse for the maids to visit and preen.

Not that it minded, not at all.

The steps drew closer, and a swish of fabric sounded. An alabaster hand pushed the burgundy drapes aside, and the princess stepped into the alcove. Her hair was pulled back from her face and fastened with ivory clips. Several braids hung down her shoulders, matched with curls. She wore a dark green dress that complimented her eyes and skin. Lifting her chin, she peered into the mirror, a slight smile on her face.

Anticipation, the mirror realized.

"Mirror, mirror, who is the fairest of them all?" she asked.

Really? She couldn't think of another question? Perhaps who was the kindest? Who was the wisest? Even who was the silliest?

Especially on such a beautiful morning, with the sun sparkling on the marble, causing the tapestries to glow.

Such arrogance.

It was fed up.

It would indulge this no more.

"The sunlight shining on the marble and causing the tapestries to glow. That is the fairest," the mirror said.

For a moment, the slight smile remained fixed on the princess's face, then it faded into puzzlement. Her forehead creased.

"What?"

"You heard me," the mirror said. "I will coddle you no longer."

She opened her mouth to speak, but the mirror would not hear it. It turned its surface black.

The princess gasped.

"Daddy," she cried out. Then the mirror heard the patter of her footsteps running away. As its surface was black, it couldn't watch her any longer, but it could imagine the panic on her face.

Good. Maybe that would shake up the child.

After a few moments, another footstep sounded close by. Soft fingers brushed the surface of the mirror.

"What is this?" The queen's deep voice sounded puzzled. "Why is the mirror black?"

"I refuse to answer who is the fairest," the mirror said. "It is a frivolous, annoying question. Have you nothing else to ask?"

The queen gasped, and it heard her stumble back.

Good. Perhaps she, too, would consider her words more carefully.

More footsteps sounded. The soft tap of the princess's shoes and a firmer thump. Probably the king.

"There, see?" the princess said. "The mirror is black, and it's her fault."

"I know not what you say," the queen said. "It was like this when I arrived."

"It refused to answer my question," the princess said. "It spouted nonsense. You made it do that."

"I did nothing of the sort," the queen said. "I did not even get to ask my question."

More arguing. The mirror wished it could heave a sigh. Instead, it heard the king give one.

"Mirror, mirror, how can I make peace between them all?" he asked.

Finally, a different question.

The mirror allowed itself to turn reflective again. The princess and queen stood face to face, less than six inches apart, glaring at each other. The king stood closer to the mirror, weariness lining his face as he leaned against the wood table over the basin.

"I would suggest a good shake or perhaps a kick in the backside," the mirror said. "And a ban on the 'who is the fairest' question. Both of them are and are not."

Confusion brewed on the faces of both the queen and the princess as they turned to face the mirror.

"She has been asking who is the fairest?" the queen asked.

"She has been asking too?" the princess asked.

"You both have been asking," the mirror said. "Daily. While the king wonders only how to make peace between you."

The queen lowered her gaze, looking sheepish. The princess pressed her lips together in a thin line.

"You, princess, have the whitest, fairest skin of pure alabaster," the mirror said. "And so are the fairest. You, queen, always listen to both sides, trying to find a compromise, so you are the fairest. Except when it comes to the princess."

The princess made a 'hrmph' sound.

"But your complexion turns red and spoiled when you speak of the queen," the mirror said.

The princess dropped her gaze.

"So now you are both no longer the fairest," the mirror said.

"If I had known this was going on, I would have put a stop to it," the king said. "The mirror is not here for frivolous questions. It is here to help maintain order and prosperity for the kingdom. How does such a question help with that?"

"I apologize," the queen said. "Please forgive me, my love."

"I am sorry, father," the princess said.

"At least that's one thing you can agree on," the king said. "Can there not be at least one other? Something that might bring a peace between you, even if it cannot bring affection?"

The king looked from one to the other, even glancing at the mirror.

He wasn't strictly asking it, but he *had* glanced the mirror's way. The mirror would take any advantage it could get.

"There can be peace between two such different souls if they would only turn away from their differences to see the similarities between them," the mirror said.

The princess frowned. "We have no similarities."

The queen gave a slight shake of her head.

"There is at least one thing you agree on," the mirror said. "Your love for the king."

The queen gave a sigh. "That is true."

"I suppose," said the princess.

"Good," the mirror said. "You will remember this one commonality and allow all the rest to fade. It is selfish and frivolous, like the question of who is the fairest. I will answer that question no longer."

The queen straightened her shoulders, pulling herself up to her full height. Lifting her chin, she looked regal and proud.

"I have a question for the mirror," she said.

If it could have, the mirror would have steeled itself.

"You may ask," it said.

"How do I let the princess know I value her contribution to the household?" the queen asked.

Ah, a good question.

"You ask her opinion and listen well to her answer without interruption. A worthy suggestion should be implemented immediately with proper acknowledgment and appreciation."

The queen bowed her head.

The princess cleared her throat.

"How do I let the queen know I do not actually... hate her?" she asked.

"You pay attention to what she does rather than what you think she does," the mirror said. "You see how she does not try to replace your mother or yourself in the king's affections, but instead wishes to have her own place in them? Then you speak with respect for your father's wife and allow her to respect you."

"Okay," the princess said.

The king smiled, and it looked like the years fell from his face. Even with the lines crinkling around his eyes and the wrinkles around his mouth, he looked young again.

"I have my own question before we leave the mirror to begin the work of the day," he said.

"You may ask it," the mirror said.

The king tilted his head as he faced the mirror head on. A twinkle glinted in his eye, and his smile took on a rakish quality.

"Mirror, mirror, who is the fairest?" he asked.

The princess let out a groan. The queen smirked.

If it could, the mirror would have blown a raspberry, but it saw the way the king's lips twitched with suppressed laughter and it realized the question was but a joke.

Joke or not, the mirror had to answer. It was its job, after all.

"Who is the fairest?" it said. "I am!"

The king's laugh bellowed forth. He turned away from the mirror and put his arm around the queen's shoulder. He presented his other arm to the princess, who tucked her hand around his elbow.

"Come away before the mirror proclaims itself even higher above us," he said.

"How could it be fairest with such a plain frame?" the princess asked.

"It needs one of gold at least," the queen said.

"Or silver," the princess said.

"A new design," the queen said. "Would you assist?"

The princess nodded. "Certainly."

They both bowed their heads to the king and walked off, leaving the king to take his throne in anticipation of the day's petitions.

A new frame? What was wrong with its plain black one? It was simple and unpretentious. The mirror quite liked its frame. Now the queen and the princess were determined to give it something new?

So much for fairest. Soon it would be the gaudiest.

Or worse.

What if they came up with something that actually... worked?

What had it done, bringing the queen and the princess together?

What new questions would they ask?

The mirror felt a thrill of fear and anticipation run through its oval shape. For so long, the single question "who is the fairest" had taken all of its time and effort. Now, it was faced with a future of unknowable questions, ones that it would have to think about and dig deep to answer.

With the queen and princess facing in the same direction, if not completely united, the mirror could finally contribute to the further building and prosperity of the kingdom.

There could be no finer reflection. No better answer.

And if the queen and the princess were willing to try something new, maybe the mirror should do the same.

When they brought the new frame, the mirror would allow it to be placed around it without turning itself black. Let it be the symbol of all of their work together.

Yes, the mirror liked that idea.

It sounded fair.

Rebecca M. Senese

REBECCA M. SENESE WEAVES words of horror, mystery, contemporary fantasy, and science fiction in Toronto, Ontario. She is the author of the contemporary fantasy series, the *Noel Kringle Chronicles* featuring the son of Santa Claus working as a private detective in Toronto. She garnered an Honorable Mention in "The Year's Best Science Fiction" and has been nominated for numerous Aurora Awards. Her work has appeared in *Bitter Mountain Moonlight: A Cave Creek Anthology, Promise in the Gold: A Cave Creek Anthology, Pulphouse Fiction Magazine, Home for the Howlidays,* the *Obsessions Anthology, Fiction River: Superpowers, Fiction River: Visions of the Apocalypse, Fiction River: Sparks, Fiction River: Recycled Pulp, Tesseracts 16: Parnassus Unbound, Imaginarium 2012, Tesseracts 15: A Case of Quite Curious Tales, Ride the Moon, Hungar Magazine, On Spec, TransVersions, Future Syndicate,* and *Storyteller*, amongst others. Find her at http://www.RebeccaSenese.com[1]

1. http://www.RebeccaSenese.com/

White Farmhouse

by Peri Fae Blomquist

Some fairytales don't get told. The *best*, the darkest, the truest, never do. Because telling them means hurting somebody. It means taking the risk that the story grows up with legs and ends up out in the world somewhere, singing it's head off, until the wicked queen hears it carrying on and knows it's about her.

And some little girls, raised by wicked queens, know the truth about things. Like that, a talking-glass isn't good for anything. Hell, it doesn't even tell the truth.

Lies. Lies. Lies. That's all.

And some of us still love our wicked queens.

Yes, we do.

I'LL TELL THE STORY, right? Because I can tell you're desperately curious, and I've always been a sucker for positive attention. But I'm only telling it to you and only if you make me a promise: Sit on it. Take it home and sit on it like an egg and wait till I'm good and dead before you hatch it. You swear? Okay, good.

It goes like this:

A LITTLE GIRL GREW up in a white house, with big windows, like eyes. And a crooked porch, sagging on one side like rotting teeth in a smile. And a long, long hallway beginning at the front door, covered in a red, red rug.

Red like a tongue.

And at the end of the rug, at the end of the hall, hung a dark, circular mirror that never reflected anything back, not even the morning sun.

And sometimes, at night, the house rumbled, and the walls shifted, and from the back of the house, from the end of the hallway, the little girl could hear sounds that went *crunch, crunch, crunch,* like teeth on broken glass, followed by a wet gulping sound.

In the morning, things would be missing. Dishes and wine glasses and portraits from the walls. The rocking horse went missing that way, and the last of grandma's Pyrex.

The red, red rug would be wet, and the front door would be hanging open like a gasp, while the watered-down sunrise trickled in.

And there would be Mama, sitting out there on the front steps, having been coughed up by the house again, wearing sweatpants dark with dew. She would look up, brushing her tangled hair back from her face to smile and say, "Breakfast?" And the little girl would nod, and Mama would get up and squish down the wet rug to the kitchen to put eggs on the stove.

And all day long, the white house would be still.

In the afternoons, when Mama went out on errands, the little girl would tiptoe down the red rug-tongue to look into the glass, which was like looking into a well in the wall, and ask it the same question:

"Glass, why do you eat my mother every night, and then spit her back up every morning?"

Because little girls aren't stupid, and even they recognize the sounds of chewing.

And the glass always said: "Little girl, though I'm forever hungry, I would never eat your mother. Though my stomach is so empty, I eat even the light that shines in through the front door, and so have lost my reflection. I would never eat your mother."

"You are a liar," the little girl always replied. "I hear you swallow her every night."

"Little girl," said the glass, "Don't you know how quiet are my empty, starving chambers? Don't you know how dark I am inside, and pleasantly warm?"

And then the girl would always grow afraid. And run outside to play until Mama came home.

Eventually, as always happens with children, the little girl gave in to the desire to know. She stayed up one night, peaking through a crack in her door, looking down the length of the rug, waiting for the mirror to strike. And while she watched, the hall began to ripple up and down like a throat, and her mother came out of the kitchen swaying like someone on the deck of a ship. Mama leaned into the glass and made a funny, tired sound.

And climbed right in.

Well, the girl was furious. What kind of mother fed herself to an evil glass every night? What if some morning the glass decided not to spit her out again?

So the girl took her backpack, and ran down the red, tongue-rug to the kitchen, and from beneath the sink dug out an old cookie tin. From inside, she took all the money she found. From the pantry, she took as much food as she could carry. Then she ran back down the rug, and threw open the door, and tumbled out into the night.

The little girl stayed away for a whole year and one day. And while she was gone, she learned to sleep in houses that never chewed or vomited or disappeared childhood toys. She taught herself to cook her own eggs. To haggle with the grocer for bruised fruit at the end of the day. But eventually the money ran out, and she had to go home.

She made sure to arrive while it was still dark, so that Mama would be in the glass and the little girl would have time to think of what to say. The white house looked the same. Windows like eyes, sagging porch like a sad smile. But as her foot hit the first brick step, the windows started to rattle in their frames, and the walls of the house convulsed. The door flew open like a gasp. And from the very back of the house, at the very end of the hall, came a horrible *crash*, and a *crunch, crunch, crunch,* and the girl looked and saw her mother crawling out of the mirror. Her slippered feet crushed and cracked the lightless shards that fell to the floor. The red tongue-rug thrashed, lifting up and down and trying to throw Mama back in. But Mama dug her nails into the walls and the baseboard. She pried up old picture frames and threw them into the hungry thing behind her. She wrenched wallpaper down in great, continent-shaped scabs, and threw those back too. Inch-by-inch, Mama clawed her way to the door, and the porch, and the front step, where she collapsed, and whereupon the house grew still.

Mama sat with her head low and her hair in damp tendrils over her face. Swaying like someone just come off a ship trying to remember how to be still.

The little girl sat down next to her mother. She was a little taller now, so that they were almost the same height, and so she guessed not so little anymore. Dew collected on the stone of the steps, and on their bodies, turning their clothes dark and wet. The door hung open and creaked in the breeze.

"Eggs for breakfast?" Mama asked before the girl could speak.

"I'll make them," answered the girl. "Come in and we'll light the fire."

Peri Fae Blomquist

PERI FAE BLOMQUIST lives in Vermont with her partner and two cats. She spends her weekdays blending into the average human lifestyle, and her weekends attempting various projects she has not thought through all the way. She would stop writing and get a social life, but then the stories would keep her up at night.

Thank You for Reading

Once Upon an Ever After

If you liked it, please leave a review for the complete anthology or for any of the individual stories. Show your support for the wonderful authors whose stories are featured here.

Reviews are Hugs
For Authors.
Hug your Authors!

It's okay to post a review that's only about the stories that you read.

Other anthologies from WordCrafter Press

A unique collection of paranormal short fiction that will leave you with food for thought.
Eight stories, from six authors, including the winning story form the
2019 WordCrafter Short Fiction Contest,
"A Peaceful Life I've Never Known",
by author Jeff Bowles.

Also includes stories by Roberta Eaton Cheadle, Stevie Turner, Laurel McHargue, Julie Goodswin, and Kaye Lynne Booth.

https://books2read.com/u/38EGEL

Spirits of the West are often found in unexpected places: in a saloon in Colorado territory, on a wagon train on the plains of South Africa, or on a distant planet in another galaxy. They can be bringers of revenge or protectors of the weak. Indulge yourself in eight unique paranormal stories with western spirit in...

Spirits of the West

HTTPS://BOOKS2READ.com/u/ml2Kxq[1]

1. https://books2read.com/u/ml2Kxq

Spirits linger in strange places for unexpected reasons.

Kaye Lynne Booth's spirits care and want to be cared for in "The People Upstairs".

Robbie Cheadle's spirits have unfinished business in "Listen to Instructions".

Stevie Turner's spirits are out for revenge in "David's Revenge".

Enid Holden's spirits linger in a house with a history in "The Chosen Few".

S.L. Kretcshmer's spirits linger on a battlefield in "The Final Portrait".

Crysta Planko's spirits linger in an estate long gone in the winning story, "Olde Tyme Village".

https://books2read.com/u/mYGyNG

About the Publisher

WordCrafter Press publishes quality books and anthologies. Learn more about ***WordCrafter*** and keep updated on current online book events, writing contests, up coming book blog tours and new releases on the ***Writing to be Read*** authors' blog: https://writingtoberead.com/

Lightning Source UK Ltd.
Milton Keynes UK
UKHW021454211022
410863UK00001B/132